KARINYA

Karinya

A novel
by

PAUL DREWITT

Adelaide Books
New York / Lisbon
2020

KARINYA
A novel
By Paul Drewitt

Published by Adelaide Books, New York / Lisbon
adelaidebooks.org

Editor-in-Chief
Stevan V. Nikolic

For any information, please address Adelaide Books at info@
adelaidebooks.org

or write to:

Adelaide Books
244 Fifth Ave. Suite D27
New York, NY, 10001

ISBN: 978-1-953510-19-8

Printed in the United States of America

Contents

Chapter One

As light dawned on the Aboriginal township of Karinya, the crows that usually encircled the sky sat patiently on the front fence; their heads turning left and right, blinking profusely in the dusty air.

There had been a party the night before and the smell of half cooked meat still lingered as two dogs devoured what remained from the fringe of a camp fire. There was little movement amongst the rubbish, soiled mattresses and crushed beer cans, only the dogs and the occasional toss and turn amongst a pile of blankets hoarded together to protect them from the night air.

"Kirra, bring me the radio!" screamed Aunty Diane from beneath the blankets.

Her request was met with silence and the stillness of apathy. It could have been a scream for help, a dying request as such or just a bland statement out of thin air. It mattered not as there was no sense of priority in place to differentiate the importance of any want or need, just a varying tone that dissipated into the cold morning air.

I was the youngest sibling of the Yunupingu household. At just 17 years of age I was often tasked to look after my Aunties and Uncles and whoever visited the house at random.

This could be anywhere from 10-20 people at any time who often drank and slept wherever they collapsed. I had a room to myself that I often shared with my boyfriend called Banjo. He was a Yolngu boy who came in from Arnhem Land for six months a year to enjoy the conveniences of metro Darwin and to escape the madness of the continual binge drinking that poisoned his community. When the lights went out at night I locked my door and barred the only window, then ignored any requests before 7am for my own safety. Banjo was there of course, not sure what I'd do without him.

The door swung open, I was half dressed and transistor radio in hand.

"Aunty!" I cried as I looked among the twenty or so people sleeping in the lounge and front yard. Some had a dusty pillow and torn blanket for comfort whilst others bore the full brunt of dirty concrete, resting their heads on the camp dogs as they breathed in and out intermittently so as not to wake their masters. It was a common site that brought sheer dismay to any visitors, especially the government authorities who were in and out before any issues could be addressed with certainty. It was a world unto itself; a life of pain and misery, apathy of the human spirit and any real understanding of what living really meant. It was the darkness I dreamt of, then awoke to find it was real, living among the helpless with a cold sense of reality that lingered in every crevice of my being.

When times were tough, my family stuck together, often using a common Aboriginal word for family (mob) "you mob, you mob" when things got out of control, screaming the word out loud to calm the moment, although with the frequency of drunken and violent behaviour, it often fell on deaf ears. No matter how bad things were, no matter who was in the house or how many police visited in one night, we always stuck together. I was unsure if this philosophy was beneficial or counterproductive, but accepted it as Aboriginal culture and a way of thinking positively in the face of adversity. Whilst it was no antidote for the heartache, it did serve as a sense of belonging and brotherhood.

"Aunty, where the hell are you?" I said, searching through the countless bodies that lay passed out on the front lawn, lifting the end corner of each blanket to cite a familiar face. By this time, some men had awoken and were stumbling around to gain a place next to the fire that had burnt out long ago. It was a time to recover from the night before that saw three of the family arrested for brawling with the Clayton mob on the adjacent footy oval.

"Here love, over here" said Aunty Diane emerging from a corner end of piled blankets.

She took her place beside the lukewarm embers and sat cross legged, beckoning for her radio to awaken the senses and perhaps distract her mind from the torment of the night before.

"Good on ya love, can you get us some water? I've got a dry shit mouth from last night. Did you sleep ok?" asked Aunty Diane.

"As always" I said, tilting my head.

I didn't tell Aunty about the constant harassment I endured after dark in my bedroom. I often awoke to the sound of men trying to push the door open with their shoulder, blind drunk without reasoning or good intention. I laid staring at the ceiling hoping the lock would hold and the cupboard that I pressed against it would not move. It was almost a daily occurrence, but with Banjo with me I felt safe.

"Fuck of you mongrel bastards!" he would say to the mob after countless failed attempts to get into my room. He often smashed the back of the door with a baseball bat to let everyone know he meant business, although this sometimes aggravated the situation. A violent response to a violent situation was all that Banjo knew, passed down from grandfather to father, father to son. He was a product of his environment and survived the best he knew how.

"Take a seat love, I'll need you and Banjo to go to the shops soon, we're all out of milk and bread" said Aunty Diane as more of the family and their fiends awoke and took their place beside the fire, that was now being relit with a match and paperbark.

"No worries, can I have some extra money for breakfast? You know how quick food goes when I bring it home. One loaf of bread and a litre of milk won't feed all this mob. The food van won't be around until 3pm so I'll need a feed" I said.

"Do the rounds and ask for a few dollars at the shops, it's the quickest way" said Aunty Diane looking up with sorrow in her eyes.

I hated begging at the shops and knew that if I was caught it was certain banishment for a week. Sure, it was the fastest way to get a few extra dollars for a feed, but the indignity I suffered as a result made me feel numb, way past the point of embarrassment. I was just a kid and already subjected to the lowest level of poverty that existed in the western world.

"Kirra" said Banjo from inside the house.

He always asked of my whereabouts in a discerning way without too much fuss. Just my name was enough to get the attention he was after.

"Can you ask these fuckers to go home or wherever they came from? They're taking up the whole living room and the place smells like shit" said Banjo.

"Aunty, can you tell them to leave, it's not safe with this many people in the house" I asked.

"They're sleeping darling, what harm can they do?" replied Aunty.

I gasped then shut my mouth. They had it over Aunty big time. The men were the ones who lit the fire and came to the fore when trouble raised its ugly head. She couldn't fend for herself with her wonky hip, bad kidneys and pleasant disposition. She couldn't and wouldn't hurt a soul.

"Leave 'em be sweetheart and go the shops like a good girl" said Aunty.

"Ok then you tell Banjo. It's not my fucking house" I whispered under my breath.

I was always very careful not to swear at Aunty Diane or any other Aunty around at the time. They were the Mothers of the emotional world, helping out when our real Mother was off site or out of the picture. With a few Aunties around you couldn't go wrong. Strength in numbers was an unspoken mantra.

Banjo was now sitting with the men by the fire. He liked one or two of them, but not many. They were drunks who took advantage of any good situation, included myself who he protected like a guard dog. He'd be going back to Arnhem Land in two months so I'd have to think of another plan or perhaps end up like the other girls around here. I looked afar at the next camp along and saw three pregnant girls around my age. I knew their names but I couldn't recall at the time. They'd been raped at some stage without a single report to the authorities, not a whisper to the cops or any government official. This was the norm at a ripe old age of 16, so I'd been lucky for at least a year. That's probably why there were so many fellas hanging around, staring at me, whispering, nudging with a sharp dagger look here and there. The only thing that was in their way was Aunty and Banjo, although he was still young and she was old and sick. There would come a time where I'd need to fend for myself and I was fucking ready for it, although I knew I'd lose, just like the mob afar with bellies like jelly, ready to give birth to yet another community member awaiting turmoil and a life of inflicted pain. I hated my fucking life and I wanted blood, I just didn't know whose. I just needed an excuse.

"Here's four dollars, off you go. Get bread and milk" said Aunty in her best voice.

Banjo stood from a cross legged stance without his hands touching the ground, something he was always applauded for. It was a way of showing his athleticism in the company of fully-grown men.

"Let's go by the mangroves Kirra, the back way" said Banjo with his head pointed upwards to get my attention. Banjo had a strong connection with nature as did all indigenous people. He enjoyed the feel and smell of the earth, and so did I.

We walked down through the salty leafed mangrove trees and into the thick dense mud that covered our feet up to our ankles.

"Squishy there babe, don't go left. Follow me this way" he would say.

I trusted him implicitly, without a hint of doubt or a single gesture of inhibition. He loved me, although he'd never say it in front of anyone and that included himself, so I guess I'll be waiting for that romantic moment for a while. I'll just fantasise with myself in the mud. Probably as good as it'll get.

We approached the back of Woolworths Nightcliff and jumped the fence with mud caked on our feet and the smell of salty leaves on our shirts. We hadn't taken a shower that day or the day before, but that was the norm. We didn't care as it was the least of our worries.

"Give me a hand bro" I said to my mud clogged boyfriend who had already jumped over the fence and left me alone.

"Just checking the scene, all clear" he replied.

I popped my head over the fence and saw a few friends from the Bagot community. There were a few good folk around here living in either community or urban housing. I always hassled Aunty to find a house in suburbia but she wanted to belong to a community, even with the constant turmoil and heartbreak it spawned.

I jumped the rest of the way down after climbing with my toes clung to the hex nuts that secured each panel. I turned around and saw a few people who we often went shopping with, both with and without money. When times were hard, I did what I had to, and that meant stealing and begging if necessary. Survival was my first instinct to satisfy. Everything else was secondary.

We walked down the back alley of Woolworths and saw a few long grass countrymen looking worse for wear. This was the terminology for full blood homeless Aboriginals. They'd been sleeping out in the cold air without any creature comforts and looked starving, sick and emotionally numb. Their eyes were yellow with Jaundice and could hardly move. They needed care, but so did I. I'd seen it all before so I just kept walking.

"Hey budda you got dollar?" said one of them to Banjo with his hand out.

"Me too bud, I'm skint" he replied with a sympathetic tone. Banjo was always polite to anyone who had it worse than him, except the violent ones who invaded his personal space.

I could see the back of Banjo as he sped onwards; his bare feet scraped along the gravel and his hands moved to the rhythm of his stride. I liked the way he walked and the intricacies of his manner. He was a good-looking fella. He liked me as well, but he didn't say anything and neither did I. We just stared at each other from time to time and kept our views a secret; at least until we smiled and had a late-night kiss when the mob had settled. It was the only time I felt special.

"Hurry up fuck ya" cried Banjo as he quickened his pace. He didn't mean to be rude, it was just the lingo around the neighbourhood. I think he loved me, but I didn't really know what love was.

"Coming, Jesus! If you'd helped me over the fence like a true fella I'd be up with you. Wait!" I cried.

I caught up and we both smiled. Even though onlookers thought they'd witnessed a domestic, it was just normal daily interaction. It was how we were brought up; it's what we saw and heard from the beginning, and it's how we are now. Only the power of self-determination could turn it around, or so I'm told at school by the teachers who had everything they could ever hope for. Let's put them in my situation for a month and see how they cope. Fucking self-determination, words for academics who've got it all. They wouldn't know that the fuck their taking about.

We entered Woolworths through a back-exit door and scanned the environment. We only had four dollars to buy milk and bread so any additional food needed to come from begging money. It wasn't something I liked or planned in advance, it was about meeting basic needs.

"Remember you've got to look desperate. They won't give me a dime but you look more vulnerable, so you're up" said Banjo.

"What the fuck, you need to do this shit too, it's not all on me" I replied.

"They're more likely to give a girl a few dollars than me. I come across as a big burly ass" said Banjo.

"Burley! What the fuck is that supposed to mean? You're just wanking out of this situation." I said.

I could see that Banjo was rearing up, most likely caused by my 'self-determination' I guess. I knew that shit would only get me in trouble.

I backed down, as always, but only because I liked him. I guess he's worth giving into. If he wasn't then who was? I took on nearly anyone who fucked with me. It was how I survived.

"Righto who then? How about that rich bird with the real estate logo on her shirt. She looks like a winner" I said.

I brushed my short cut brown hair with my fingers and practiced my best smile into thin air, then turned to Banjo and shrugged my shoulders.

"What? Just do it, come on!" said Banjo.

I turned and walked towards the lady, then saw my reflection in a shop window. I looked bad man, like a woman that had just slept in total fear of her safety and hadn't eaten any breakfast. I looked better than the long grasses out back, but not much. I wondered what my chances were of getting anything in my current state.

As I drew nearer, a stabbing pain began to throb in my guts, my throat began to swell and I sneezed twice. The lady looked nice; well dressed, well-mannered and seemed to have everything she needed. She looked calm, I looked desperate and I wondered if I needed to quickly change my outlook if I wanted to be successful. I wasn't good at this and had failed miserably beforehand. I talked using my best English.

"Excuse me, I haven't had any breakfast, could you spare a few dollars?" I asked with complete trepidation in my tone. She looked at me for a few seconds and seemed to take pity, or was perhaps thinking of how to say no without offending me or making a scene. In that split second in time, I knew she'd say no by the look in her eyes that was a mixture of empathy and embarrassment. It was all interpretation of course, but I knew it was a lost cause.

The lady shook her head then looked around to see if anyone she knew had seen her, most likely her friends or clients, then shrugged her shoulders and smiled downwards at her shoes. This was one of the reasons I chose people like this as if I was rejected, the polite sort would always keep their discontent hidden and not DOB on us to security. Sometimes we couldn't pick and choose. Begging seemed to be an art form with little reward as nothing could compensate for the loss of dignity and the embarrassment in the moment. Even if they handed over a hundred dollar note instead of a measly dollar, it wouldn't have changed anything. Money can't tame emotions, only supply fleeting moments of joy and a band aid for the real issues at hand.

Banjo had already seen my dismal failure and was talking to a lady at a stall. She was selling tickets of some sort. I walked into Woolworths and bought a loaf of bread and emerged to find him sitting on a bench.

"Where's the milk?" I asked.

"I bought a lottery ticket instead" replied Banjo as he glanced sideways, hoping that I'd miss what he said.

I stood in front of him and thought of something to say. He'd spent the milk money on a ticket for fucking whatever and he didn't seem to care.

We were in the middle of a supermarket so I didn't raise my voice, although that hadn't stopped me in the past.

"You stupid cunt. You know what that money was for. Show me the ticket" I demanded with a firm tone.

I snatched it out of his hand and held it up to the light. It was an all expenses overnight stay at the Mirambeena resort in town with $200 spending money. It was to be drawn tomorrow morning at 8am in the mall and the winners notified immediately.

"I asked for two dollars then she got the same amount out of me for the ticket. Pretty smart bitch" said Banjo.

He wasn't referring to the lady as a bad person, just running off the many scripts in his mind that formed his sense of expression, supported by an average vocabulary that got the job done. With our level of education and the adversity we faced, it was what it was. I was the same. Did I want things to change? Sure, but how would that happen? And who the fuck cared? I didn't know. But what I did know is that each day flowed into the next, and the challenges kept mounting.

Banjo got up and walked out the same way we came. I followed as usual.

"You stupid Mother Fucker, how are you gonna explain this to Aunty?" I said with a somewhat sympathetic tone.

I feared for his safety, as I did for mine. If something happened to him then I'd be vulnerable. I wondered if this made me selfish.

"Didn't you see who that girl was at the counter? That was Anna Wilson, my old Maths tutor at Bayview College.

She said she'd work it for me"

"You're fucking kidding me?" I replied.

"Two nights all expenses paid stay at Mirambeena with some cash. It'll be drawn tomorrow, and then we should hear some good news. Worth the investment?" Asked Banjo.

"Are you sure? Why would she do that for you?" I asked.

"She owes me one" he said.

"What for?" I asked.

He replied with an evil smirk. A common gesture to imply a deep dark secret that only his heart would divulge, or not! Anyway, it was before we met so who gave a fuck. Well, actually I did but that was my script when I needed self-assurance and a way out. It was an easy option and I did it a lot.

"You still need to explain the milk situation to Aunty, and you can't tell about the ticket as everyone will want to come and stay" I said.

Banjo looked down to the ground as we walked out the back doors and across the car park. The scene was almost identical on a daily basis; shoppers doing their thing with a variety of people mixing in harmony: mothers with prams, tradies on a break and a few oldies from the retirement village down the road. The community folk seemed to stand out though as we looked poor and desperate. It wasn't something I thought about all the time as meeting basic needs was more important, like being safe, eating, and sleeping out of the rain, but I must admit I wanted to be normal, and so did Banjo. Perhaps this turn of events would do just that?

We couldn't think of anything to do so we climbed the nearest Mahogany tree to see things from a different perspective. It was times like these where high places made me feel good, away from ground level dwellers that pushed their views on me and looked at my clothes with contempt. To go high was to escape. We got half way up the tree and looked outwards across the Nightcliff area. The high-rise apartments and million-dollar housing estates all surrounded my community which had next to nothing. It was a distinct contrast to see the shiny reflective windows of million-dollar apartments against a backdrop of mangy dogs and houses with no doors. The class distinctions were in such close proximity that one only had to look out the window or peer over the fence to see a world unto itself. An invisible world, shunned by most; its surroundings bright and colourful with the dark urban shadows existing between the lines; a world just as real, just not as brightly lit.

"I'll just say I lost it and take the heat" said Banjo after trying his best to come up with a smart solution.

He never tried to gloss things over with a bullshit useless answer, just how it was in simple terms. He made sense, well, to me he did.

"This won't go down well though, we'll need a back-up plan for the night if things get rough"

I nodded in agreement. I knew what he meant.

We arrived back at Karinya ten minutes later to find everyone in the shade. The sun was up and the heat was searing in from all angles. It was November so the wet season humidity was on the rampage, floating in at ground level at 98%. Even the dogs were sweating. Aunty noticed at once that something was amiss due to the fact that we'd been gone almost an hour.

"Did you forget the milk?" Asked Aunty Diane.

Banjo had a response all planned out but it never eventuated.

"What happened, I need that milk" said Aunty with a concerned voice.

In moments like these, it only takes a raised voice or a series of quick nervous moments to start things rolling, and Aunty had provided the spark.

"Get back to the supermarket" said a man sitting by the fire in a loud voice.

Another man disliked his tone and threw dirt in his direction. Another threw an empty bottle and the mood turned from placid to volatile. In slow motion, I could see the brains and gore of my community shut down.

Banjo tried to make them sit down but was struck by another from behind with a closed fist. Banjo quickly removed his shirt and wrapped it around his fist then punched him in the face. Banjo was a street fighter from way back and knew that his hand would not stand up to the force without protection. The man went down but there were others to take his place. They sprawled out onto the adjoining footy oval with sticks, rocks and their fists, and fought until they collapsed. The older members sat back in the shade bellowing their discontent which fell on deaf ears.

"Great out of there you mob" cried someone.

"No peace here, all humbug day and night" said a woman by the fire.

The mood was sickening, loud and violent with blood spilling onto the soft grass where a footy match would play out that very afternoon.

There was nothing to do but wait until reasoning kicked back in and common sense prevailed. This was a daily occurrence in the community but sometimes played out in public places like the supermarket or the beach. It was like any fight; sometimes you won and other times you got pummelled. It was then time to go to hospital and line the hallways with the injured, often taking up one quarter of the hospital at any given time with violent related injuries.

It was a time to recover and meet other countrymen from communities in Darwin that experienced the same situation but in a different place. It was a time to rest but not necessarily reflect on the reasons why it occurred. This simply didn't happen as the underlying causes were etched into our subconscious like a tick that's taken hold for the long ride.

"Kirra, fucking help me" cried Banjo lying down behind the goal posts. He'd been beaten senseless with a cut above his eye and a swollen cheek bone. They had attacked him from the front and behind. It was his initiation to manhood and motivated by jealously. We were a couple and they knew we had sex. They wanted me like those other pregnant girls around the camp fire. Fuck em, I'd rather die.

I didn't reply to Banjo as I knew that when he laid down and asked for help they'd back off, which is just what happened.

As worthless as those guys were, it was an unspoken rule not to hit a man when he's down. Of course, this depended on how much alcohol had been consumed on the night.

All in all, there didn't seem to be a pattern in the reasoning behind the violence, except the violence itself. It was like we were due for a brawl going by some kind of biological time clock or something. It could start for any reason really - no milk, someone woke up grumpy, jealousy, no blankets or alike. Jealousy was the main reason I guess; comparing possessions, girlfriends, having something that others didn't. The list went on and when a brawl was due, any excuse would do. It was just a matter of going through the motions then recovering. We would all make friends again until the next time. The problem was, this was all that ever happened with a few good things in between. People like to talk up our culture and explore all the good, and I'm all for that, but the constant anguish and downright fucking heartbreak overrides it all. I fucking tell ya, it's a nightmare in the light with my eyes wide open. I feel like crying every fucking day and often do. The only people I care for are Aunty and Banjo. Take them away and I'd be joining my ancestors on a voluntary basis, I shit you not.

I walked over and picked up Banjo from the far end of the oval after telling a few women to leave or face the consequences. They went packing and left me to tend to Banjo who had blood running down the side of his face. The others had already caught the public bus to the hospital. They'd return later that night with bandages to the head, feet and arms. Then they'd walk around the supermarket looking for sympathy. Useless wankers.

"Help me man, stop the bleeding quick" said Banjo. I had a few stitch bandages in my room, the ones they use in boxing to stop the bleeding until the other guy hit you again in the same spot. Made just as much sense as living here I guess.

"Ok bud, let's go. We'll make it to my room then hide out. Aunty Diane can you help here?" Asked Kirra.

She was in no state to help after having been king hit by an older lady with a piece of wood. She was conscious, barely, but in no mood to converse.

I managed to drag Banjo into my room, bolted the door and dragged my cupboard across the entrance. We were safe for now; at least for a few hours before the mob returned. They'd want payback at some stage, but not usually the same night. It was if the process was timed out by a higher purpose as no one ever talked about these things, they just happened like a bolt of lightning.

"Lay down, don't move. I've got ya babe" I said to Banjo as he opened his eye wide open so I could lay the stitch bandage across evenly. He was tough as nails but still just a kid. In fact, he was my age. He was my choice. Better than one of those old fucks that raped girls and got away with it. I had their number I can tell ya.

"Lay still fuck ya. There, now don't move for five minutes" was my instruction before I laid by his side.

"You're an angel man, I thought I was screwed for sure cuz. Three at a time, beating me from back to front. I want payback bro, let's get em together?" asked Banjo.

"So when does it end?" I asked.

"When it ends bruss, when it ends!" he exclaimed with his stitch almost popping from his eye socket.

"No, when is all this going to fucking end? Look around you cuz, no one wins. It's never a case of who dares wins but who can win? Look where we are now. In a few hours they'll be back and it all starts again" I said.

"Talk to Aunty" said Banjo.

"She's almost at heaven's door, no one listens anymore. She can't protect us any longer. We have to do something" I said.

"Come with me to Arnhem Land" said Banjo.

"Is it any different there?" I asked.

Banjo paused and realised why he was in Darwin. It was actually better in town than in a rural community. At least there were more police and a major shopping centre, which had a movie theatre. That's assuming we had money of course, which we didn't.

"No, I mean we have to do something about all this shit" I said. "How do you mean?" said Banjo.

"I mean, all this shit that goes on. We have to take some kind of stand. I don't fucking know" I said flapping my hands down on the bed in frustration.

"Ok, let's bunker down here and go to the shopping centre first thing in the morning. The ticket will be drawn at 8am so we can go straight to Mirambeena. That should give us 24 hrs to come up with a plan" said Banjo.

I nodded, fully expecting Banjo to come up with the goods.

"So, the best we can do is to look after ourselves? Man, my heart bleeds for this place." I said.

Banjo could only nod in agreement, thinking of all those who had lost out at the hands if their own culture. It's as if indigenous people had signed an agreement with Lucifer himself before arriving on earth.

As the night progressed we slept without water or food in our stomachs; a reminder of our predicament. I could only image what cuisine lay ahead in the resort restaurant and what new clothes we could buy with the prize money. It would be short lived, but it's better than not living at all.

All that night I dreamt of being an activist. To stand up to the injustices of the world and take action. I saw Luke Skywalker defeating Darth Vader, canoes forming a line to stop the damming of the Franklin River and Eddie Mabo with his fist in the air when he finally won his court battle. These were great people who started their crusade from a single idea, a solitary moment where something ignited inside them and said "this shit can't happen anymore" then they did something about it. That was me, that's how I felt not only in my dreams but in the daytime, frustrated as fuck and wanting to crack skull. I had to channel my fears in the right direction but I didn't know where to begin, but then again did Mabo or Skywalker? They started off with little direction, looking for answers on a lonesome track to somewhere in the middle of fucking God knows where. I had to do something, I just didn't know what. In fact, I didn't have a fucking clue.

Chapter Two

I heard a few bumps in the middle of the night as the hoard arrived back from hospital. It's usually a guaranteed seven hour wait at hospital with any kind of injury that's not life threatening, which pretty much included anything bar having a heart attack or arriving with a pick axe in your back. It was a hospital I guess but only just. No money for private health around here, just the basics which included food and water. I was hungry, thirsty and tired. I'd copped a king hit to the jaw last night as well. I could feel the muscle around my jawbone tighten its grip as I clicked it to the left and right. It wasn't the first beating I'd taken and it wouldn't be the last, especially as I grew older and was exposed to this shit environment each and every day. But I still felt strong. In my mind, I was already an activist; building a rebellion on unchartered worlds ready to fight the galactic empire, having a solid case prepared, ready for a land rights battle, or rallying the troops to stand up for the Franklin River when no one else would. I felt unstoppable even though I had no plan, no food or water, felt unsafe and had copped a hiding the day before. I had nothing, so I had nothing to lose; backed up against the wall without a care in the world of any repercussion that may arise. I had me, Aunty, friends from school and Banjo. That was enough for now. I could make this work.

It was around 6:30am when we decided to make our move. I opened the door and found only a few sleeping bodies this time, wrapped up in bandages to conceal their wounds. It was a vast improvement on the day before, but I didn't get too excited. Inherit social problems don't go away because a few people cop a beating and learn their lesson. Mr. Hyde would come calling again in the not so distant future, perhaps that same afternoon. It was time to go. I turned to see Banjo awake and ready for action. His eyes were full of fire with payback in mind. It was my job to ease the tension.

"Let's hang out in the mangroves until eight and get a drink from the tap near the fence" I said.

He didn't flinch. He laid motionless, thinking of the night before, or perhaps the day ahead. We had to move as more men were arriving back from the hospital and shit would brew again as soon as the sun warmed their heads, helping to recall the distained memories of the past.

"Let's do this shit. We deserve it Babe" said Banjo as he got up and put on a shirt.

I smiled for the first time in a week as I imagined a warm bed at the resort, nice food and perhaps some new clothes. These thoughts kept me calm as I walked out the door of my so-called home with Banjo by my side.

"I'll be back in a couple of days Aunty, we're going to visit friends in the city.

"Will you be ok?" I asked as Aunty lay on the front lawn still upset from the night before.

She didn't reply.

As I entered the mangroves, I looked back at the only home I ever knew and clicked my jaw once again, the pain still with me as were the details of how it happened. It wasn't a place where I wanted to return, or leave. There was good and bad in everything but the bad seemed to override all reasoning at this stage, aided by a swollen jaw and an image of pregnant teenagers standing around the fire. I saw Aunty get up and go into my room. She was tired and in pain. I then realised that she gave up all her creature comforts for me on a daily basis, willing to sleep on the front lawn so I could be safe and out of the rain.

I felt a warm hand take mine, and that was it. We had ventured across the threshold of perhaps no return as Banjo led me by the hand into the warm mangroves. Mud squeezed between our toes and we laughed like kids again, enjoying the sensory exposure backed up with high expectations of the day ahead.

"Are you sure you've got this all organised?" I asked. "Shit yeah, no hassle. She owes me one and it's time to deliver. Stuff all of the tickets have been sold anyway. Everyone wants to go down south this time of year." he replied.

The mud began to get softer and deeper, now up to our ankles. "Here, jump on my back, I'll carry you the rest of the way" said Banjo.

I didn't have to say a word. He knew when I was in trouble and was there in a flash. I jumped up and got mud on his shorts, then his t-shirt. I looked around at his face to see if I got a reaction. He was smiling.

"You're a dirty fucker now cuz" I said with my mouth in his ear. "Always bruss, day and night. You know me" replied Banjo. His sense of humour was a little dry, but dry martinis aren't all that bad either if there's no beer in the fridge. He was all I had in the world and I'd defend him with a baseball bat.

We stopped near the far end on some sandstone rocks; red and white in colour which smelt of fresh sea water. We ran our hands along the surface then held them up to our face. The salty sensation was a natural remedy for any unease felt at the time. The rock smelt like ochre sand and salt mixed together, a nice way to wake up and calm the senses after a night out. We placed our hands in the mud and made hand prints on the flat side of a very large sandstone rock, always side by side, little hand big hand all the way along the flat edge. They would last until the tide came in that evening, then wash away into the harbour, with memories of yesteryear joining the salt water. We were paying our respects to the salt water spirit. It wasn't polite to ask for anything in these moments, just to interact on a personal level and share mind, body and spirit.

"Last one, then we need to take off" said Banjo as he pressed his hand next to mine.

I looked at him and smiled.

"Totally wicked Babe" I said,

This was my way of expressing my feelings; a kind of 'I love you' I guess, well that's as close as it got for me. You can't expect a girl to be exposed to violence on a daily basis and still be able to express affection like other people. I didn't have it in me and neither did Banjo. We did our best with what we had and who we had become. Words aren't the only way to communicate.

We pretty much had mud all over us by the time we reached the shopping mall. Banjo had washed his shirt under the tap and left it to dry on the back fence. Males were allowed to walk around without a top for obvious reasons.

"There she is. It's almost 8am" said Banjo referring to Anna who sat in the middle stall next to the smoke shop. She saw Banjo and gave him a wink. I moved closer to Banjo and gave him a kiss on the cheek. Anna knew what it meant.

"She's spinning the wheel" said Banjo.

"What's our number?" I asked.

"Lucky legs 11" he replied.

It was no coincidence that Anna had legs that went on and up forever, her best feature by far. She was a white girl who was nice to everyone she met and never distinguished between black and white. I liked her too, everyone did.

Anna took one last glance over her shoulder to see if the coast was clear then drew his number from the barrel.

"Number 11 is the winner. Banjo Marlngurra" she said looking in their direction.

If anyone was looking closely, they would have noticed her eyes on Banjo before she chose the number. No one around here was that quick or perhaps even gave a shit. Half the population of Darwin was on holiday down South on the Gold Coast. Nobody wanted to stay at Mirambeena. Beggars can't be choosers I guess. I hated that saying.

"Fuck yeah!!" screamed Banjo as he waltzed up to receive his prize.

This was his way of showing excitement but also drew attention to him and his win, much to Anna's dismay.

"Congratulations you dumb shit" whispered Anna as he arrived at the counter.

Everyone had now turned away and gone about their business. "Thanks miss, you're a legend" replied Banjo as he took an envelope of cash and a voucher for a 24 hour stay at Mirambeena Resort. They could check in at 10am then out at 12 noon the next day. 26 hours exactly but who was counting.

Banjo walked up to me and laughed.

"Can you believe this shit cuz? Just you and me in paradise" he said.

I didn't know what to say. I just kissed him on the lips in front of everyone. I wouldn't normally do that in a public place, but this was special. This was going to be awesome. I hoped this good fortune would lead to something else, anyway that's how it works right? Success builds on success and good things always come in pairs? That was my secret wish at the sandstone rock, but I didn't say it out loud. The best wishes never are.

My wishes were my own, away from the reach of prying eyes and insidious motives. They were there to act upon in times of need, in moments deprived of humanity and self-worth. My dream was to put an end to the injustices that Aboriginal people are subjected to on a daily basis, to write the wrongs of the past and carve a new direction in the sandstone, to live as others do and have the same rights. Was this too much to ask? Fuck me, I just wanted to be human. Was I born into this world to live as an animal, or second-class citizen at best? Give me one good reason why I shouldn't take on the world and fight like a caged Pit Bull? My ancestors were here first, so where's the respect and gratitude? Is this shit I see each and every day thanks for a million hectares of land and countless atrocities? I wanted blood each and every day but I knew this attitude would eventually lead to conflict. Well actually, I didn't give a fuck, because no one gives a fuck about me.

"C'mon bruss, it's time for paradise" said Banjo from just up ahead of me.

"What do you mean I'm right here next to you? What's the hurry anyway it's only 8:30am, we can't check in until 10" I said.

"I recon I can get an extra hour out of them, especially if a room is already clean. 10am Check in time only allows for the cleaning to get done. That's one whole extra hour in bed, in a bath, watching TV and being happy" said Banjo.

I guess that's all we really wanted......to be happy. To wake up and smell the roses instead of urine on a wall or filthy dogs that licked the faces of those who slept. A simple wish that would come about if proactive change was to occur. I hadn't figured it out yet, but something different needed to happen if the word HAPPY was to be a regular occurrence in my vocabulary.

We waited for the public bus on Nightcliff road for thirty minutes with a mob from Bagot Reserve. The kids were running around the bus shelter playing chasey whilst the Moms' and grandmas' looked on. They weaved in and out of the seating then played chicken with the cars on the road, but not really. The little tykes were no more than 3-5 years old and street wise before they were even allowed near one by themselves. They were growing up like me, like Banjo and like everyone else I knew. I felt happy for them in the moment, darting in and out beneath our feet. Who knows what would happen to them in the next hour though. It was good to see them smile, if only in the moment.

"C'mon where is this fucking bus man, frying my ass on this seat I reckon" said Banjo.

"Why don't you play chasey with the kids then?" I replied. "Good idea, but I don't think the Bagot mob would appreciate me chasing their kids onto the road, there's enough trouble between our two mobs already" replied Banjo.

Even though the two communities were only 10 minutes apart, they spoke completely different languages and adhered to different law. In general, there was white law and there was black fella law. We had to live in both worlds as such. With all my moaning I actually prefer white fella Law as it's more consistent. Seems like my mob bends each law to suit themselves, although I wouldn't say that out loud to anyone for my own safety.

The bus cruised down Nightcliff road in stylish fashion as the wheels hugged each bend towards the city centre. It may have just been the fact that so-called paradise awaited us, at least compared to Karinya. The Mirambeena resort was on Cavanagh Street opposite Woolworths in the city. It wasn't really paradise as there were better motels in the area, but who was complaining. We planned to take advantage of every second there; soaking up the atmosphere near the pool, drinking foreign beer and eating as much gourmet food as possible. It was a time to be lazy, carefree and even get a small pot belly. How would we explain that when we got home? I didn't want to think about it.

We hopped off at stop 12 in the city and headed straight for the resort. Banjo was pretty keen so he pushed the entrance door a little hard and frightened the lady at reception.

"What can I do for you?" Said the lady with a nervous tone. Banjo slapped the voucher on the counter and lifted his nose in air.

"Where did you get that?" Asked the lady.

Banjo's nose came down to her eye level and stared her down.

What the fuck did she mean by that, he thought.

"What the fuck did you mean by that?" asked Banjo, saying what was on his mind, literally.

"Oh, nothing really, one moment" said the lady as she went out back to make a call.

This was a tense time for both of us. It was tempting to cause a big scene and stand up for yet another injustice, but the risk of being thrown out was very real as Banjo had already sworn at her, and she wasn't happy.

The lady emerged from out back and waited to see if we'd say something else. She waited, and so did we. I held Banjo's hand as I could see he was rearing up. We kept our cool, at least for the moment. I could see the reaction she desired was not forthcoming by the smart ass look on her face and the slight 'huh' gesture at the end of a long and arduous stare. I was so damn proud of Banjo, and of myself.

"I talked to someone called Anna so all good" said the lady. What was all good? I thought. What the fuck was all this about? Why the fuck didn't she believe us in the first place? Do all black fellas lie and steal to get what they want or something? This is the shit we have to endure 24/7 from life. It's bad enough when we get home, but to have to put up with this shit in silence was something else. It's the build-up you see; once or twice a year then perhaps I could handle it, but every week or perhaps each day is too fucking much. People wonder why we are so angry all the time.

"Hey look at the black fella mouthing off" people say. I've heard that shit so many fucking times it's engrained within my soul. I hear that voice in my sleep and relive the experience every time I open my eyes. If that bitch was anywhere else that day she would've been fried toast on an open fire, ready to feed to the camp dogs, burnt to a crisp.

"Have a nice stay, you're room is number 21, top floor on the left" Said the lady talking to the counter.

We didn't say anything, we just smiled and walked down the hall hand in hand. Being happy in paradise meant no agro, at least for now.

"I reckon that bitch was testing us. I couldn't believe I held back and took it from her" said Banjo.

I leant into him and walked as close as two people could without falling over.

"Proud of you bro" I replied.

He didn't hold back entirely, but it could've been a lot worse, a hell of a lot worse.

Room 21 was like the others on the top floor; nice and spacious with new carpet and curtains that blew in the wind with each gust that came through the louvered windows. There was a queen size bed with black and white coverings and thick fluffy pillows. There's nothing like a fluffy pillow to take the blues away; it was like hugging your best friend or a second Mum lying in waiting.

The room had its own en-suite with new vivid white towels that hung from the railings next to a brand-new vanity unit, just installed the day before. We walked the room in total awe, struggling to find the words to express our delight. We didn't take any detail for granted. There wasn't a single entity that we didn't notice, not a corner of the room unexplored or shiny object that wasn't looked at in detail. It was all new and exciting. It was normality, which was foreign land at best.

There were other couples checking in on the same floor and I tried to imagine what they were doing and their reaction to the room. I imagined a stock standard placid reaction. Simply checking into a resort as they'd done a million times before with a shrug of the shoulders to express their opinion. I wanted to be like them. I wanted to feel apathy in my surroundings like they did. But fuck that, it was a time to run amuck.

"Fuck yeah" said Banjo as he jumped on the bed.

He bounced up and down like a kid on Christmas Day. I could hear the springs begging for some respite, bearing the weight under his man size body mass that pounded the man-made structure like a wrecking ball. He gestured that I join him.

"Fuck yeah, whooo!" I said as I joined him in holy matrimony, arm in arm on a bed that was actually comfortable and didn't look like a stale piece of crusty bread with a few rags to garment. We planned on enjoying every second in this foreign environment that most took for granted. It was a time to rejoice and enjoy the moment.

"Let's take a shower babe. I'll run the water" I said. "No point if all we have are these daggy clothes to put on afterwards. I'll go down to the souvenir shop and buy a few things. We could be a pair for the day, same shorts and shirt, eh?" Asked Banjo in an enthusiastic time.

"Sounds corny as fuck" I replied.

I then looked at my clothes and noticed the mud and torn fabric, we were almost at homeless status I reckon. I nodded to him as he stood at the door, then I took a shower.

The first thing I noticed about the shower was the vivid white tiles and how they reflected in the light. I could see the outline of my body in each one that I looked at. It was the cleanest place I'd seen for years.

The water was soft and warm and the soap was fragrant. A welcome change to the outside shower at home where 'bitsa' soap was the only solvent available. This type of soap comprised the many small pieces that were too small to use on their own. When this ran out there was nothing but the cold water from the bore below. It was better than nothing.

I felt the soft warm water flowing over my chest and down my legs. The soap mixed with the water beautifully and for the first time I didn't have to scrub profusely to create any suds. My hands were relaxed as I rubbed the soap gently up and down, to and fro lifting my head to enjoy a steady stream of water, holding my head back for as long as possible before taking a breath. I felt my woes dissipate into the air, I felt at ease in the moment, unfazed by the experience that I knew would end when life returned to normal. It was better to live then not to have lived at all, or so the saying goes, or perhaps I modified it a little. In any case, love was living I guess and if this was living then I was in love.

I dropped the soap and did it all over again, wishing Banjo was in here with me. I heard the door close and he appeared with a matching pair of shorts and t shirt.

"We're tourists' babe. Look at this shit will ya?" Said Banjo as he held up a shirt with 'I've been to Darwin' on the front. "Whooo! What a thrill man, I'm a new person bro" I said as the water continued to seep over my shoulders.

"Get in here boy" I said to Banjo.

He ripped his shirt off and flung it into the bin with my old rags following close behind.

We shared a moment under the steady stream of water as I ran my fingers along his chest, sharing my suds with the only man I had eyes for. We kissed under a steady stream of water, like being under a waterfall in a blue lagoon on a far-off island in the Pacific Ocean. Our eyes were closed so anything was possible. The feeling of the water, the sound of the beads hitting the floor and his tongue in my mouth made the moment surreal in nature. I wanted that blue lagoon, I wanted this moment to last for eternity, and I wanted peace. I wanted it all, but I'd heard that line in a movie somewhere that didn't end well. I stopped dreaming and focused on the kiss. It was fucking magic.

We were still kissing in the shower when all the other guests on our floor were walking down to the restaurant for a feed. We were lost in the moment and on the verge of an interlude in the shower. It didn't happen this time as we had never fucked in the shower before; we simply didn't have that level of privacy back home. These intimate times occurred in my room behind a locked door, often interrupted by a hip and shoulder by a drunk fuck who wanted to join in. No fucking way José. That baseball bat in the corner came in very handy when the beasts came calling with a gut full of grog.

"We're here babe. We made it. Something's gonna happen out of all this. I can feel it" said Banjo as he ran his fingers through my wet hair.

I couldn't help but stare into his eyes and believe every word he said. I just nodded without even listening to a single word. It all just sounded good and made me feel happy. We were full of hope in a good situation.

We got out of the shower and dressed like tourists, then stood in front of the mirror.

"We look like dorks, a pair of dorks" I said.

It mattered not, as it was a substitute for something far less desirable; from rags to riches.

We walked down to the restaurant past that bitch at reception and took a seat at the far end table. With our new clothes and clean skin we passed as tourists from interstate, or perhaps urban black fellas who came from a respectable background. I don't think the receptionist even recognised us when we passed by. That's the power of first impressions I guess, but what the fuck could we do about it? Rig a lottery and spend the prize money I guess, and that's exactly what we did.

"Prawns babe, look streak and red wine" said Banjo with excitement in the air.

"Soup for starters, let's go easy" I replied.

"Soup, fucking soup! No way bruss, let's hop into this shit and eat" whispered Banjo.

"Try to act civilised. You don't want to draw attention to yourself again" I said.

"Why not? We're only here for a short time so let's dig in" replied Banjo.

We ordered prawns, chicken, steak and stir fry all at once. The table was chock as with food, not even enough space for a knife and fork, let alone a wine glass. We skipped the alcohol for that very same reason and perhaps the fact that we didn't want people staring at us whilst we drank. Even if we had one wine we'd be classed as alcoholics on a binge of some sort. It's just what people thought when they saw black fellas with a can of beer or a glass of wine. We'd drink later at our room.

"Try this babe" I said as I placed a prawn on Banjo's plate. He picked it up and ate it shell and all. He closed his eyes and enjoyed the crunch as the shell mixed with the meat. This was the traditional way to eat shellfish, at least where we came from. Sharing food at the table was common place in our community. If one person had food then all would share, if someone had money then we all had money. As fucked up as this concept can be and the amount of trouble it caused, there was still something cultural about the whole thing, and to be immersed in culture gave me structure in a world that made little sense.

We ate into the night and ended up sharing a bottle of wine when the restaurant was empty. We didn't usually drink so it went straight to our heads, losing all inhibition and fear about what the future held. It's ironic that we stayed away from the drink, but we saw what damage it could do to the lives of so many others, so we decided to stay on the straight and narrow. As we got older that could change of course, and it usually did.

We couldn't eat another bite and sat back in our chairs with a temporary pot belly. The type that went away the morning after a binge, so I guess it wasn't a real one. We looked at each other and asked the hard questions of ourselves without saying a word. Our thoughts were a collective of the here and now mixed with the future. The meal was good and we had new clothes, but what would the feeling be like at 12 noon tomorrow? All the glamour, shiny spoons and pleasant mannered waiting staff wouldn't change what lay in store when the bell stuck 12 the next day. Was all this shit just a band aid solution to our problems, or perhaps respite at best? Most likely the latter.

"Let's go upstairs and fuck" said Banjo.

"You can't ask me any better than that?" I replied.

"Nope" he said sipping on a glass of lemonade.

What the fuck, I didn't care. What was I suddenly passing myself off as a well-mannered lady or something? This was who he was and he spoke how he did.

"Fuck yeah" I exclaimed as we hopped up and walked hand in hand to our room.

As we passed the lady at reception she glanced our way, noticing our hand in hand walk to the room. I could tell she was jealous, perhaps not of Banjo but of getting laid. She looked hard up. Fuck her.

Banjo turned off the light as soon as we entered then flicked the button to the air conditioner. This was a must in the Darwin wet season where humidity can reach 98% in the day or night. To have sex without it meant a homemade swimming pool of sweat between the sheets. We'd done it before, but even my bedroom at home had a working air con; it was a necessity like meat and potatoes for dinner.

"Give me that shirt Babe. I'd like to see that whistling clean body of yours" said Banjo.

I didn't reply. I just held up my hands with a willing disposition and a seductive smile. Within a few minutes we were between the sheets kissing with our tongues, feeling our way through the night. He reached down and caressed my vagina with his penis and leaned over me.

"Where the fuck is your condom?" I asked.

"Let's live for the moment cuz, can't you feel the emotion?" Replied Banjo.

"Fucking no way boy, didn't you learn anything in sex Ed classes at school? Safe sex bro" I said with a discerning voice. "Fuck those teachers, most of them were banging each other anyway" he replied.

"Yeah so what, how do you know they weren't wearing condoms?" I asked.

He didn't reply.

"Go downstairs and buy a condom from the vending machine at reception" I demanded.

"No way, that bitch will see me. Ah who gives" said Banjo. The need to get laid overrode everything else at this point. He strolled down to reception in just his shorts. The other lady had gone and a hot shit white girl had taken her place. She looked like a hooters barmaid with an elegant twist.

"Can I have a condom?" asked Banjo.

She pointed to the vending machine on the wall and smiled. "Have you got anyone to use that on big boy?" She asked in vain. Her humour was not welcome, but Banjo didn't care. At least she was only joking, not like that fascist slut before her.

One hour later they were curled up in each other's arms pretending to smoke a cigarette. The sex was good, as always. I rode Banjo like a hungry cowgirl with vigour and a sheer willingness to please. When I had sex, I gave it everything I had. I loved him, so why not.

Our heads lay together on one pillow as we talked up each other's performance. There was nothing worse than spoiling the moment with a comment like "I've had better" or alike. I wouldn't do that to Banjo, nor he to me.

I began to rub his stomach way down below as usual after the fact.

"These sheets are soft. I can't stop wiggling my toes" I said. Indeed, the sheets were soft, made of pure cotton with a warm blanket to seal things off. We were in paradise, another world unto itself from the other side of the planet. A nice place to be for a while.

"I miss Aunty and our friends from school" I said.

"Hmmm, we haven't been to school in a week, the boys will be wondering where I am. I'm not calling them or they'll come over and run amuck. I'll call 'em later tomorrow. Turn on your phone and see if you have messages" said Banjo.

"Na fuck it, it's our time I reckon. They'll always be there but we won't always be here" I replied.

"The only reason I go to school in the first place is to socialise. I mean, when school ends what are we gonna do?" asked Banjo.

"Just hang out I guess or try to find a job" I replied. "Find a job, did I hear you right. The national unemployment rate for Indigenous people in this country is 47%. That's almost half of us and it definitely includes around 90% of people in communities like ours. Half of us can't even speak proper English" said Banjo.

47% of indigenous people in Australia were not working as of the 2016 national senses. I studied this at school in social studies. The reasons are vast I guess but no one has a solution. My heart bleeds for this country, my heart bleeds for me.

"I don't fucking know, what can we do?" I said.

"Fuck knows, just running out a statistic, that's all" replied Banjo.

I laid there motionless, still, and peaceful trying to fathom what had just happened. Could I do something about it?

I was always taught at school that one person could make a difference, and that the power of one is grossly underestimated.

"Do you know of any other statistics?" I asked.

"Possibly, actually most definitely if it's related to Aboriginal people. We've had the shit end of the stick for a while now, you know that" replied Banjo.

I didn't tell him what I was thinking at this point as I wasn't sure myself. There was something brewing inside me though, a stabbing pain in the guts like when Eddie Mabo found out that Murray Island in the Torres Straight was crown land, then decided to do something about it. I didn't know if I would use his measures or one of my own, but something was swelling within my gut in sheer desperation, and whatever the outcome was, it would likely be adverse.

Chapter Three

"Do you have any smokes?" I asked lying next to Banjo. "Nope, but they're for sale in the lobby. Our tab is still healthy I reckon" said Banjo.

"We'll both go, let's get some exercise" I said.

We arrived at the lobby at 9pm to find the front counter unattended. There was a supermarket across the road so we strolled across to Woolworths to get some smokes. We couldn't smoke inside anyway and I needed some exercise. From across the road I could see a bunch of countrymen lying on the footpath waiting for a bus. I didn't know what mob they were from but they were visiting Darwin by the looks, as their 4WDs were dirty from the ride into town, perhaps Port Keats or around that way?

We walked past them and gave our best wishes.

"Eh how are ya budda?" I said to one of them.

"Where your mob from?" He replied.

"I'm Karinya mob, he's Arnhem mob" I said pointing to Banjo.

We stopped and sat with them for a few minutes.

The bus pulled up and two young women helped their grandfather to the door. He was blind and had severe jaundice (yellow eyes). He was crook and needed help.

"No way, you're not getting on here, too much drink grandpa" said the driver.

"No blind, he blind" said the young women trying to get him on the bus.

The door shut in their face as onlookers sat in silence. I remember the faces of those in the back seat of the bus, looking back at the old man as it drove away, and the tears he shed with yellow eyes aflame. 50 metres down the road there was a young couple drinking VB cans with their mob. They got into an argument and started to yell and scream at one another. The family tried to stop their bickering but to no avail as violence once again took hold. He grabbed her by the arm and flung her to the ground, then curled his fingers through her hair and dragged her across the road. She screamed with pain as her back scraped across the rough bitumen. To and fro she slid with no end in sight. Her t-shirt began to tear from the constant barrage of alcohol fuelled violence as the whole family spilled onto the road to break up the fight. This made things worse as the men and women then took sides. The violence consumed the entire road; the squelching of faces being punched; the sound of hair being torn out by the roots and the harrowing screams of the women as their family was torn apart before their eyes. "Get outta there you fuckers!" was all I could say at the time. They weren't my mob or skin clan, so I didn't get involved. Perhaps that was the problem. The only ones who could stop this mob violence were the cops and they didn't show for another forty minutes.

Banjo took my hand and led me away. We bought some smokes and an iced coffee then had a smoke outside the front entrance. It felt good to smoke after sex and to relax after seeing violence. It calmed my nerves and made me feel real again. It was a luxury that I couldn't afford so I asked my mates for a smoke most of the time or scrounged butts from the ground to get one or two drags. This was common place in Darwin as fags were bloody expensive. A pack of cigarettes costs around $17. I often went halves with a friend and bought the cheapest brand. These were usually packs of 40 but they were shorter and thinner so it all evened out.

Banjo exhaled in the air and walked back around to see if the Port Keats mob were still there. All he saw was a sea of blue lights and an ambulance that had just arrived on the scene. The blue flashing lights made all feel at ease. The cops were the only ones with any influence around here, depending on how long they took to arrive.

"Same shit everywhere bruss. Let's get back to the resort and have some peace" said Banjo.

I nodded in agreement and flicked my cigarette into the gutter. It still had a few drags left on it, so I knew the countrymen would salvage the remainder later that night. It was a disguised form of generosity.

The front entrance to the resort was blocked with police cars so we went around the back of the supermarket to enter from the other side. As we approached the large skip bin at the back Banjo stopped to pick something up off the ground.

"Fuck me it's a gun, oh no it's a toy" he said waving it around.

It had an orange tag on the top to indicate it wasn't real so there was no need to panic.

"Let's have some fun with these Port Keats mob" said Banjo as he removed the orange tag and began to wave it around like the Oklahoma Kiddy in a John Wayne classic.

"Fucking yeehaw! I'm the Oklahoma Kiddy. Watch out you fuckers on the road" said Banjo.

Unfortunately some of those fuckers on the road were police. To make it worse he was seen by a few countrymen on the footpath. "He got weapon, he got weapon" they cried.

This was a catch cry for anyone who held a stick, rock or anything that could do more harm than a naked fist.

The police shone their spotlights down the alley and saw Banjo jumping up and down pretending to be on a horse like the Oklahoma Kiddy.

"Banjo, you did put that orange cap back on, didn't you?" I asked.

"It's in the bin, why?" replied Banjo.

"It's how everyone knows it's a fake. Throw the gun away, quick" I said.

But it was too late. The police had already seen the gun in his hand and took no chances. Four cop cars sped up the alleyway with their sirens blaring. The front car made an announcement. "Put down the weapon and lay on the ground with your hands on your head".

We quickly ducked behind the bin to hide before panic set in.

"What the fuck, what are we going to do?" I asked Banjo. When times got really tough, I looked for his guidance. I would always back him up with whatever he decided. He was my man.

"Fucking run!" replied Banjo.

This was his plan. It was either flight or fight mode and to flee the scene seemed logical. It was four cop cars versus us. I don't know what the cops expected really. It was better to run I guess than take on the cops with a fake gun. We wanted to live, but wondered whether life after death would be any better.

"This way babe, quick" said Banjo.

He was pointing to a gap in the fence behind the bin. Most fences in Darwin are made if corrugated iron and made a hell of a racket when bumped in any way. We had to squeeze in and out pretty quickly. We both cut our legs in the flurry of movement and left a trail of blood for the cops. It didn't last for long, but it was enough for them to know we'd been hurt. The cuts weren't deep but they stung like fuck. The last thing we heard were the countrymen on the street shouting

"They're Mirambeena mob, they from there".

The cops wouldn't take long to find out where we'd come from as the bitch at reception would surely give away our identities. A quick call to Anna would be the only thing left to do before they converged on Karinya and stormed our room within hours.

We sped across the lawn of a house then jumped several fences before we stopped in an alleyway to catch our breath. "What the fuck was that?" I asked with my hands on my knees panting.

Banjo shook his head unable to find the right words. He stood tall, placed his hands behind his head and walked around. We were tired, really tired. Most people think that we're fit as we walk around the bush a lot and play footy, but it's not the case. We're like anyone else that doesn't exercise and eat good food.

"We need to get to Jimmy's house in Larrakeyah. We can stay there until the heat cools. We need time to think" said Banjo.

"Whatever, I can't think. You lead" I replied.

We ran and ran until we couldn't move anymore, arriving on the front lawn of a half decent block of units on Houston street, about half way down. We were still visible from the road and could hear the cop car sirens blaring in the distance. There were people standing on their balconies trying to see what the commotion was, then looking left and right down the street to see any action. It was like entertainment to them, not really knowing what the issues were and the emotion and heartbreak that followed. Some were eating popcorn and drinking coke.

Was I in a movie? Fuck, was I a movie star? I wanted to shoot them where they stood.

We sat up on the lawn once we'd had a breather.

"Let's get up to Jimmy's. The light is on, he's always home" said Banjo.

Jimmy was an ex Bagot boy. He'd grown up on Bagot reserve which mirrored their own community, and had experienced just as much pain and anguish as them. He'd let us in.

We climbed up to the top floor and softly tapped on his back window.

"Jimmy, Jimmy it's me, Banjo" he said. "Jimmy let me in, c'mon man open up".

The curtain opened slowly from one side as a pair of eyes protruded from the darkness, staring down the pair with an inquisitive look. Jimmy had heard of their adventure on the radio as the pair had already been broadcasted across Darwin as being armed and dangerous.

"Be on the lookout for a male and female of Aboriginal appearance. Last seen in the city wielding a gun at police. Do not approach them as they are armed and dangerous" said the radio broadcaster.

The back door opened slowly and Jimmy appeared. He was a tall thin fella with a shaved head and a moustache about the same age as them.

"What the fuck is going on? Why did you come here?" Asked Jimmy.

"You've gotta help us man, we're in big fucking trouble bruss. We need somewhere to hang out for a while" said Banjo. I held my hands up to my face and tried to hide, then slapped my thigh quickly after and began to cry. How could paradise turn to hell in such a short space in time?

Banjo turned around and saw me crying then turned back to Jimmy who was clicking his jaw left and right. He was thinking.

"Did anyone follow you?" asked Jimmy.

"What sort of fucking question is that? Of course, someone followed us, can't you hear the sirens?" replied Banjo.

"I mean, to this house stupid. I'm not letting you in only to have my door busted in an hour later" said Jimmy.

Banjo adjusted his tone to appear more calm.

"It's cool bro, we lost them in the alleyway. We just need an hour or so, that's it" said Banjo.

I let him do all the talking whilst I played the lost damsel in the woods routine. This seemed to work.

"Ok get in, hurry up" said Jimmy.

We slipped in quietly and left him at the door. He looked around outside for a few seconds before closing the door softly, bolting it shut from the top.

We took our place in the lounge room. I'd stopped crying at this stage.

"Thanks Jimmy" I said.

"Yeah no worries" said Jimmy with a hint of sympathy in his voice.

He was a Seinfeld fan and was half way through episode 5 of the second season. His book shelves were crammed with DVDs which kind of defeated the purpose of having book shelves, but anyway what the fuck. It was his house.

Jimmy had been unemployed for all of his working life, if that makes sense. He took a few hits early on and was convicted on several break and entering charges. This stuck on his rap sheet so no one will touch him. He's in a major fucked up situation that 50% of indigenous people find themselves in, compared to 25% of non-indigenous people in Australia. That's half of us without a job, and no real hope of getting one.

Crime is then an easy option, but I guess you've heard it all before. Fuck I don't know, what do you do?

"What are you going to do?" Asked Jimmy.

"Keep running I guess, the black fella way" I replied.

"The black fella way, what does that mean?" Said Banjo.

He could have sworn at me but he refrained.

I realised that I'd made a racist statement but I thought it was ok seeing as it was my race. Banjo disagreed.

"You can always hand yourself in?" said Jimmy.

This statement was met with complete silence. We didn't want to get locked up, that would make things worse. Banjo's father was an Aboriginal death in custody case so he hated jails of any kind. He would rather go down swinging than be cuffed and locked up, and so would I.

I then reflected on our journey thus far; the winning ticket, the many insights I had about being an activist and the peaceful moments that I enjoyed thinking of how to better my situation. Do people really know about indigenous issues and understand them as injustices that we all have ownership over? Probably not I guess. Was apathy a solution? No! Were harsh laws an antidote? Definitely fucking not! Then where to go? What to do from here? It was fucking killing me. I then saw something in Banjo's pants and no, it wasn't his cock.

"Why have you still got that gun?" I asked Banjo, seeing it poking out of the back of his pants.

"A souvenir perhaps. I don't know, does it matter?" Replied Banjo.

"You fuckers are crazy man, I shit you not" said Jimmy, trying to listen to what we had to say over the TV.

"Look, it's really fucking simple. You have two choices: give yourself in and cop the consequences or keep running. By the sound of it you choose the latter, agreed?" said Jimmy.

We nodded at the same time.

"Right then what's the plan? You can't stay here forever. I can hear the sirens from here man" said Jimmy.

Then I said it. "50% of indigenous people are unemployed"

"Yeah so what?" Replied Jimmy.

"Well, how many people actually know that? And how many actually give a fuck?" I asked.

They didn't reply. I didn't think Jimmy knew that himself. Jimmy and Banjo looked at one another then stared at me. I was staring at the ground.

"We need to turn this bad situation into something worthwhile. We can't just get pinged for this and spend time inside the clink. We may as well make it worth our while" I said.

"You're making me fucking nervous" said Banjo.

Jimmy agreed.

"I'll say it again, slowly. 50% of all indigenous people are unemployed" I said.

"So, what do you want to do, shout it out from my balcony and tell the world?" asked Jimmy.

"Yeah, awesome solution" I said in return.

I was going to give it to him for his smart-ass comment but this was his place and we were in it.

They weren't getting it so I grabbed the toy gun from the back of Banjo's pants.

"Hey, that's mine, Jesus give it back Kirra" demanded Banjo. I held it up in the air like Oklahoma Kiddy and pointed it at Banjo.

If I repeated the same line now would you remember what I said"

"I dunno" he replied.

I stood in front of him and yelled.

"Do you know that 50% of all indigenous people are unemployed?"

He looked down the barrel of the pistol and swallowed. He got the message. We had to spread the message across Darwin. We had to make this situation count.

"What the fuck is that? Exactly what will that achieve and what difference will you make to the situation?" asked Jimmy.

"You want us to be terrorists to educate the public on Aboriginal issues" asked Banjo.

"Look I don't fucking know. We have to do something Banjo. Don't you see? This shit just goes on and on and fucking on forever. We need to take a stand" I said.

The activist inside me was taking over. I was finally exploring my inner self and coming up with a solution, however skewed it was. I agreed, that scaring people to get a bit of publicity was bad, dumb and illegal. But I was backed up against a wall each and every day and I knew the two fellas in the room with me felt the same.

"So we get pinched and get locked up? Is that what you want?" I asked Banjo.

He shook his head and thought of his father.

I didn't want to use emotional blackmail on him to participate in something he didn't want to do. But I was desperate to fulfil my destiny, and willing to use whatever arsenal I had in my limited bag of skills.

By this time, Banjo was calm. He had seen things my way deeply influenced by his Father's death. He sat there motionless, staring at the carpet. Jimmy could see his reaction to my lecture and turned down the TV.

Banjo was only 12 years old when the news got back to Arnhem Land that his Dad had hung himself in a holding cell in Darwin. The shit faced guards didn't remove the bed sheets, thinking they were depriving him of comfort. He tied one end to a bar on the window and the other around his neck and pushed the bed away. They didn't find him for an hour. His Mum got all the payout for that. He didn't see a dime. Really bad fucking situation. Cut him deep I'm telling ya. I felt like saying sorry but I didn't want him to change his mind. I felt like a bad person, perhaps I was.

"So we use the gun to create awareness of indigenous issues? How?" Asked Banjo.

I was thinking out loud.

"We pretend to rob a liquor store. We don't take the money as that would defeat the purpose. We take maybe, a dollar let's say. We then leave a message at each place like '50% of all indigenous people are unemployed' or something like that. This would then get back to the media" I said.

"Stop, this is terrorism man I'm telling ya" said Jimmy. He then stood up and grabbed the gun, broke it into three pieces and gave it back.

We'd thank him for it later.

"Ok then, we'll hand ourselves in and take the heat" I said. All nodded in agreement. It was the logical thing to do and made sense. So why did Banjo and I look so fucking miserable?

We started to watch the TV as conversation drew to a close and heartache set in.

"Change the channel please Jimmy" said Banjo as he hated Seinfeld. Then it happened, as if my thoughts had jumped into the TV and came to life. It was 11pm and the channel 9 news came up on the screen.

"Police are investigating an abduction of an indigenous female by gunpoint earlier this evening. She has been named as Kirra Yunupingu from Karinya community. Police say the suspect, Banjo Marlngurra has taken her hostage and is at large in the Darwin area. He is described as being Aboriginal, dressed in a white shirt and armed and dangerous. Please do not approach this person under any circumstances. Report any sightings to crime stoppers on 1800 767 000" said the reporter.

We sat there stunned, trying to think of something to say, anything really.

"Hostage? Where did that all come from? Lying fuckers" said Banjo looking around for sympathy.

"You're in the shit big time bro" laughed Jimmy.

"Fuck you bruss, it's my head on the block here" said Banjo. "I didn't make you pick up the gun and act like a juvenile Cowboy" replied Jimmy.

"No, wait, this sounds good. If I'm a hostage then I'll be free if we get caught" I said.

"Oh my, mother fucking Teresa. I'm in!" Said Banjo. Jimmy laughed.

"No, this way we won't be hurting anyone. We just go on the run and make our point at each place. For example, I write the unemployment statistic down and give it to Jimmy. He waits until we've left and calls the cops and the media. When they come he hands the message over and talks to a reporter about his problems. It then gets to the papers to raise awareness. When it's all over I'm Scott free and we'll try to get you off as well. Is that still terrorism? I asked.

"Not far off, but a hell of a lot better than sticking a gun in someone's face." replied Jimmy

Banjo simply nodded. He was all out of ideas and didn't want to talk.

"If I do this for you, what's in it for me?" asked Jimmy.

"It's to raise awareness, to fight for indigenous rights, your Aboriginal, get it?" I explained.

Jimmy took a drag of his cigarette and exhaled. He was a pretty bright fella, more than he let on. I could see his brain ticking over as he looked at me with squinted eyes and smoke coming from his nose. He was saying yes to me with his mind, I knew it.

"Hmmm, alright but would I be breaking any laws?" Asked Jimmy.

"Probably, but they're after us, I don't think they'll waste any time on you" I said.

Jimmy thanked me. He took my statement as a compliment.

And so it was decided; we go on the run and make a stand at each place highlighting a different issue. Someone then dobs us in and the media arrive to beam it out into the community.

"So are we all in?" I asked.

"Sure, what's the worst that can happen?" Asked Banjo.

"You could all get locked up and the key thrown away" said Jimmy.

"Perhaps, but I don't think so. I've got a good feeling about this. There's always risk in everything" I said.

This is what I was waiting for. That spark inside me was now a burning flame, the activist that I saw within me was now alive. I could now not only fight for myself but create awareness for my people. There was uncertainty, that's for sure. The cops already had Banjo on an abduction charge and they could also ping our friends for aiding and abetting a criminal. We could get a lot of people in trouble I reckon. But fuck it, you get one chance at greatness each lifetime, and this was mine.

"Ok what are you waiting for man, get the Fuck outa here. I can handle myself" said Jimmy.

He was getting worked up as he now saw a cause to fight for instead of watching TV all day until he fell asleep. It wouldn't change his situation much as his rap sheet and unemployment history pretty much secured his fate. He could now see the worth in helping others that came after him. At least that's what we thought. He'd be ok.

We crept out the back door as Jimmy called the cops and media. We didn't hear what he said but we trusted him. We hid in the garden next door for only 10 minutes before we heard the first siren. Pretty soon there were five cop cars and a news crew on the scene. It was good to see them for once, we just hoped that Jimmy would be ok.

We saw the cops arrive and the media talk to Jimmy on the front lawn.

He passed them the envelope with the unemployment statistic and they took some photos. We told him to mention his long unemployment history at the same time. We hoped this would work and catch on, but the cops could have put a privacy block in place. We weren't sure. The whole thing took about 40 minutes, then it was all over. We couldn't talk to Jimmy so we fled on foot. We ran down Mitchell Street then down to Cullen Bay beach. This was a place for the rich but not so famous. Anyway, it was a private place to rest after all the commotion.

The night air was warm and the sand was soft so we curled up under a tree and fell asleep. It wasn't the first time we'd slept on the beach. We just needed to watch out for the green ants. They were real little pricks that latched into your leg. Not a nice way to wake up in the middle of the night.

We woke up with the sun as usual and took a walk to the Cullen Bay shops. We had money and nice clothes so one of the alfresco diners let us in, usually they wouldn't. We ordered toast and coffee and bought the morning newspaper.

"Holy fuck" I said in a subdued tone.

"Look Banjo, its Jimmy on the front cover and his story" I said.

Banjo began to snigger as he read the headline.

'Larrkeyah crusader fights for Aboriginal rights' was the headline. The article about Jimmy went on to talk about his employment woes with their statistic included, and a background story of how the hostage crisis unfolded. It was fucking magic. There wasn't much worth reading in the NT news at the best of times so this was a welcome change.

I was surprised they got the story in on time. Nothing happens quickly in Darwin.

We ate and laughed at the picture of Jimmy with a sad face and hoped this story would make it national across Australia.

"I just hope Jimmy's ok. He's stuck his neck out for us" I said.

"Looks like it worked. Glad he took the gun off us then" said Banjo.

"Fucking oath, what was I thinking?" I asked.

"Prison time babe, prison time" Said Banjo.

And he was right. Anyone who sticks a gun in someone's face deserves jail time. I'd learnt my lesson, but I was desperate and seeking a quick solution. I then wondered how many terrible decisions were made in a desperate state of mind, and how things would have been different if they'd taken the time to think. Emotional control is a god sent.

We sat enjoying our second cup of coffee, staring out onto the water when we noticed other diners staring at us. Were we famous already? Did someone want our autograph? We looked up at the television and saw pictures of us on CCTV behind Woolworths. They were clear and showed Banjo holding a gun then pulling me through the fence. It was time to leave, but it was too late, the owner had already called the cops.

"It's alright love, they'll be here in a minute" said the owner as he stared at Banjo with the look of the devil. He was the bad boy and I was the angel. I kind of liked that I guess but I showed him some sympathy anyway.

"Let's go Banjo, there's a cop station just up the road" I said.

We could already hear the sirens from afar. We jumped into the water and swam under the wharf, in and out between the pillars to avoid detection. We were good swimmers, getting lots of practice in the surf dodging the jellyfish and crocodiles. Well, maybe not the crocs, it sounded good though.

We stayed under the wharf and swam to the end where it got shallow. We saw a small truck pull up and deliver some packages so we jumped in the back if that and pulled over the tarp. It started to move pretty much straight away, moving slowly towards the northern suburbs, or so we thought. We travelled for about 20 minutes then popped our head out the back for a look. We were in Parap. This was an upmarket suburb with leafy trees and nice cars parked in each driveway. As the car stopped at a traffic light we jumped out as quick as a flash. A Greek guy then got out shouting "Ella, Ella" which means come back, I think. The Greeks rebuilt Darwin after the big cyclone in 1974. It was a big fucker, category 3 on Christmas Day of all days. I respected the Greeks for staying and helping to rebuild the city. And, for the free ride of course.

We fled on foot to the Parap pub and went out back into the car park. We immediately saw someone we thought we knew.

"Fuck, it's Aunty Nat" I said to Banjo.

"Is too, let's go" replied Banjo.

"Aunty Nat, Aunty Nat" we cried as she got into her car after a lemonade at the local.

She wound down the window.

"Jesus Christ, your pictures are all over the news, and the paper. Get in here before someone sees you" said Aunty Nat.

Nat was a school teacher so she didn't like to swear at all. She talked slowly and used proper words. I liked to listen to her run off a nice sentence or two and secretly wished I spoke like her and not like a rough community girl. It's not that I don't like myself, I just think things could be better, don't we all?

Chapter Four

We sped out of the Parap Pub looking like bank robbers. Nat, who usually drove slow and careful, was hooting at cars and using the right lane to speed past any vehicles that were obeying the speed limit.

"Slow down Aunty" said Banjo.

"This isn't like you" I said.

"I need to get you two home and out of sight. The whole community is talking about you. Banjo do you know you've been accused of abduction?" Said Aunty as she sped down the road towards her home in Jingli Gardens.

"Here come the cops, you two down" said Aunty.

There were two paddy wagons coming from the opposite direction. These were modified cop cars with a jail attached to the back. Any person who required detention were thrown in the back and locked up. I've seen people chucked in head first by the cops for vagrancy. It must be a hard job but there's no need for violence, especially as cops are supposed to be role models of society. Much like Aunty Nat I guess, and that's exactly what she was; a role model in every way. She looked after anyone who needed a hand. Not financially though as she wasn't made of money, but she lent a hand whenever she could.

I didn't see her much as she wouldn't come anywhere near our place. Can't blame her.

We ducked down and held each other's head to the floor, just as they drove past. They were looking for someone with intent in their eyes, ready to draw the baton or whip out the capsicum spray. They were under pressure for an arrest, and the longer this went on, the more intense it would become. Soon they'd set up road blocks around Darwin to get a result, which usually worked. The city was only so big with a couple of ways in and out, not like a big city by any means. We needed friends and family to support us, and that's exactly what we had, although we'd find out friend from foe in the coming days.

Aunty drove into her house in the half decent suburb of Jingli Gardens. It wasn't posh by any means but well looked after by the community. She was born into a poor family then removed at an early age by the government under an assimilation policy at the time. Not really sure what to make of it all as it was so long ago and I don't know all the facts. I wanted to talk with her about it, and I guess now was a good time.

"In you two. You'll need to spend the night here as there are cops everywhere" said Aunty.

She had never invited me into her house before, but I guess this was a special reason, or perhaps she agreed with my cause and wanted to contribute. I planned to dig a little deeper and see what I could find.

"Thanks Aunty, appreciate everything" said Banjo with his head bowed entering the door.

This was a mark of respect. We all knew when to mouth off and when to hold our tongue. There were distinct unwritten rules to follow in certain situations. It's hard to list them all but we all knew. It was now time to show respect in

Aunty Nat's house, and to do whatever she asked of us. Anyway, we needed her help.

"Get the BBQ ready you two. Here's the oil and every-thing else you'll need" said Aunty.

She went to the fridge and took out a few buffalo steaks and several goose fillets. These rare Darwin delicacies fried up well on the BBQ. The Goose needed some marinate though to ease the gamy taste, so Aunty had made a traditional com-bination of orange juice, olive oil, mustard, sugar, soy sauce and honey. We wanted to slurp down the marinade by itself as soon as it came out the fridge. Really good shit I'm telling ya.

Pretty soon the word had spread as Darwin is a small place. We had visitors from all the surrounding communities as well as urban folk who were in total support of our cause, although they were all aboriginal at this point. I needed the support of everyone. There was more work to be done.

Our pictures were now all over the news, both locally and nationally. The newspapers had supported us against the cops' advice. They told them that publicity would only encourage more of this type of behaviour, most likely com-paring us to terrorists. We weren't demanding anything of anyone; simply creating awareness of the issues at hand in hope for change.

One of the visitors that day was an ex politician. He took me aside and told me the politicians weren't happy and had talked to the top cop to get a result, and fast. People were calling into the NT news to ask about us and whether the stat on unemployment was correct. The newspaper had verified that it was indeed correct according to national statistics. I had a few others up my sleeve to share before this was all over. I felt empowered, perhaps even self-determination played a role. Whatever it was, it felt good.

I missed Aunty Di, although I knew the others at home would've told her about me and Banjo. She couldn't read or write like most of my family; just the basics really - filling out forms and alike. This was the norm. My literacy levels weren't flash either. This was common place right across the board with most five-year-old Aboriginal children not attending pre-school. It all starts from there and if you miss the boat, it's hard to catch up. This means low literacy skills. Being educated is empowerment. Without it, it's like waiting for a boat that you know will come within a week, but you can't ask when or tell the time to find out yourself. The only thing you can do is wait. Really frustrating I reckon. My heart bled for Aunty Diane.

The term Aunty is a little confusing to outsiders. Basically, every Aboriginal woman who's older than me is an Aunty, so the family structure increases 100-fold, depending on what kind of relationship I have with each person. If things weren't good with Nat, then she wouldn't have helped us. It's kinship at its best, but has its pros and cons.

"Ready Aunty" said Banjo as he lifted the steak and goose from the hot plate.

It was done to perfection with a few crusty edges on the buffalo fat, but that's how Nat liked it so we cooked to her preference. I made a potato bake which is my absolute favourite dish. The creamy taste of potato and cheese really does it for me. I felt comfortable even though I was a wanted woman, well actually it was Banjo they were after but he didn't care. We'd started something now and it was time to follow through.

We ate once then we ate again, all the time wondering if this act of generosity was linked to kinship or respect for standing up for our race. I think the two go hand in hand as people and issues go together. I kept looking at Nat the whole time and she just smiled back. I think she was happy to see me happy and eat something other than dry bread or off milk for lunch. It was her payback for a lifetime of having it much better than I. Perhaps she felt guilty. I kept smiling at her.

Later that night we sat watching TV with the blinds drawn. The cops were a bit slow and would take their time getting here. We knew they would come eventually as half of Darwin knew we were here. It goes to show the level of division that existed within the community as info travels fast, but only in certain circles.

We chatted about certain things that made us feel good as Aunty didn't want to create unnecessary agro after all we'd been through, but avoiding the hard issues only leads to more problems later on. I put my crusader hat on and cleared my throat.

"Aunty, tell me about when you were young" I said.

She quickly ran off a short spiel of her life in high school and how she played sport at the state level. This was a script of some sort and I wanted to dig deeper.

"No I mean before that, when you were young, a little toddler" I said.

Aunty froze. All the happiness seemed to drain from her soul like a squeezed orange awaiting the bin. She didn't flinch, just stared at the TV without a response to my question. The atmosphere changed from lukewarm to an Icelandic winter. I felt like I was standing on the end of a Jetty in Iceland looking out onto a frozen lake of memories that needed to be cracked with an ice pick. I wasn't qualified to do so, but neither was Banjo.

"It's ok Aunty, she's just digging" said Banjo.

I gave him a look of contempt, like 'shut the fuck up' or something, but I would never say that to him.

Aunty took a deep breath and swallowed again.

"What do you want to know?" she said.

"Tell me where you were born and what you did for fun" I asked. "Well, I was born in Darwin, just on the outskirts in a kind of shanty town. We didn't have much, just the basics" said Aunty. She glanced at us with a darting look as if the niggling info was yet to come. In a split second, with just one glare in our direction, she was trying to push out a memory of old that had been suppressed for many years.

She froze yet again and swallowed.

"I was taken away when I was three and sent to live with another family. They were kind and looked after me. I got an education and food was always on the table. They said that my family couldn't look after me properly, but I was too young to know that for sure. I remember the day though, as clear as you two sitting here now; it was a sunny morning in the dry season when they came. The government sent whoever they could muster to gather us kids into a truck. They pulled me from my mother's arms and said I would see her again. I never did. I remember driving away and hearing the wailing of my Mother and seeing her hands in the air, moving to and fro with grief, slapping herself in the face and body. She too was removed from her mother so she knew what it was all about. Everyone lied to us with smiles on their faces and daggers in their shorts. Some came with batons even though only a few were policemen. The job was so big they needed reinforcements from the community. I cried for months afterwards. I cried for me, for my Mum and Dad and for my Brother and Sister. I knew that ill feeling would flow into the next generation, but what could I do? So here I am an educated woman with nice food in the fridge and a good house. I guess I need to thank the government in some way, but I don't really know what I missed out on, although when I see the kids at the park with their Mums playing and laughing I can take a good guess.

That's all I have to say about that" said Aunty with tears flowing down her cheeks.

I felt guilty, really fucking guilty. Banjo just sat there thinking of his father and how he took him fishing in the river in Arnhem Land, until disaster struck at the hands of the penal system.

I took a deep breath, I too with tears coming down from the corner of both eyes, ever so slowly running down to the end of my jaw bone.

I opened my mouth then closed it again. There was nothing to say. I had another statistic in my notebook some-where that I'd started since the fever of activism took hold in my brain. I took it out and flicked through the pages. There it was; a national statistic on the stolen generation of Australia.

I showed it to Aunty who nodded.

"Where did you get this from?" she asked.

"Various places, mainly from school. Banjo is the one who showed me the first few" I said.

"Yep, too right, they're all above board" he said.

I nodded, although I knew that any statistic could be questioned. There was room for interpretation and so-called justification of the circumstances. But the real evidence lay in the very dispositions of the people who were there and the tears that flowed like wine from the eyes of those affected. I realised that I had to do something, people needed to know, or perhaps to only jog their memories. I went over to Auntie's desk, wrote down the statistic and placed it on the coffee table.

It read:

Almost half of Indigenous adults reported that either they or their relatives had been removed from their natural family.

I looked at Aunty to explain the drill but she already knew. "I know, DOB you into the cops and call the media, then talk

about it on camera. I read it this morning in the newspaper"
said Aunty.

"You don't have to do it Aunty, we can find someone else"
I said.

"No, it needs to be said. I can do it" said Aunty fighting back
the tears.

She was brave and would need to tap upon her strength to
get the words out at the right time. Our cause depended on it.

Banjo went outside to take a piss even though there was a
perfectly good toilet inside the house. This was his community
habit and Aunty didn't try to stop him. She just smiled, until
she heard the sound of pee making contact with her well-man-
icured lawn and the smell that drifted in the front entrance.
I closed the door before she could say anything, turned off
the porch light and sat next her. She giggled and slapped my
leg softy to cheer herself up. I was there for her if she needed
someone, just like she was for us.

"Pigs!" Cried a voice from the front lawn.

I quickly got up and opened the curtain to see a cop car
out front. They'd caught Banjo with his pants down, literally.
There were two of them, dressed in blue with a bullet proof vest
and a standard issue revolver.

Banjo zipped up his pants and made a move for the front
gate which was blocked by the thinner cop who obviously
worked out. The female police officer stayed in the car as she
was only a cadet. She'd get some experience today I can tell ya.
Nothing like learning on the job.

"It's over Banjo, come with me" said the cop.

The image of authority, a blue uniform and a gun made
Banjo see red. All his aggression usually tied back to the painful
memories of this father. He received no counselling for this
and as a result the anger manifested into pure rage each and

every time he was challenged. I've seen it so many times in my community. The brain just shuts down, literally, and the pain and anguish of yesteryear takes hold in the form of verbal abuse and cold hard fists.

"Come on you white cunt. Come and take me bro. You're not a man, you're a pig, a sticking fucking pig" said Banjo to the officer. He was trying to antagonise him, and it worked. The cop came running at Banjo with this hand on his baton like the old white cops of South Africa in the 50s. He didn't move and was rugby tackled to the ground and slammed onto the grass. I saw red, bright fucking red and ran out front to Auntie's objection.

"Stay in here love, you'll get hurt" said Aunty.

I didn't respond. I was too angry and Banjo needed me.

"Let him go you white fucker" I said out loud as I walked up and down the lawn.

I didn't mean to be racist but it's just what comes out when the brain isn't working and the only language that's used is in scripted form. It's the same each time really and swear words make up a large part of each sentence structure.

"Go inside miss, you'll get hurt" the cop said to me.

I continued to pace up and down the lawn watching them both wrestle like Gorillas. They got to a stage where they were both standing so I jumped on the cops back and pulled his hair, what there was to pull anyway. It was an ugly scene but the cushioning of the soft grass made it easier to bare when we fell over. Meanwhile, the cadet cop was in the car calling for backup. She wouldn't come out for some reason, and had decided to block the driveway with the car, thinking that we couldn't jump a fence if we wanted to.

I kicked the male cop in the balls from behind which slowed him down, significantly. As he lay on the front lawn in the foetal position I looked at him and hoped that he'd be ok. It wasn't him that made me angry, it was the fact that he was standing in front of my dream with a sign saying 'it's over baby'. Fuck that, it's over when I say it is. Can 200 years of oppression be silenced by one king shit cop with an apprentice who wouldn't even get out of the car. I was stronger than that.

We stood on the lawn for a few seconds and looked back at the house. Aunty was crying, holding the envelope with the statistics inside. She knew what to do next.

The cadet was still locked up inside the car so she was no threat to us, but she was blocking the entrance to the driveway. In the distance we heard the sound of multiple cop car sirens and knew it was time to leave. I waved goodbye to Aunty then we both jumped onto the bonnet of the cop car then into the street.

We ran down the middle of the road for around 500 metres, watching the curtains open and close in the many households that recognised us. Some opened their blinds to see fugitives, others to see a pair of heroes who had the guts to stand up for something. Everyone had an opinion, but we had ours as well and that's all that mattered. Were we activists or terrorists? You decide.

At the 250 metre mark we diverted into scrubland which slowed us down, big time! The feeling of sticks and stones under our bare feet was nothing new, but it meant that we needed to walk instead of run. We heard the sirens blaring in the distance; a long wailing sound followed by short intermittent high-pitched tones. It could have been an ambulance for the ball trodden cop on Auntie's front lawn, but more likely back up cop cars coming our way.

It wasn't unusual to experience ups and downs in our life. It was common place. Just today we'd been eating marinated goose with Aunty Nat then wrestled a cop two hours later. This was the life of an Aboriginal person trying to live in an urban world with problems to sort by the handful. Peace one moment, violence the next at the flip of a coin. There was no use complaining though, we had business to finish.

"Were does this path lead?" Asked Banjo as he found a narrow track with soft sand.

"There's a block of housing commission about 50 metres ahead. I think Abigail lives there with her foster kids" I said.

"Do I know her?" Asked Banjo.

"She's your cousin man, Abigail from Casuarina!" I explained.

We had so many cousins that we didn't keep in touch with. Not like the usual three or four in Darwin and a few down south. We had loads, too many to count. We didn't talk to all of them, but we knew each other by site. Hopefully Abby had read the newspaper or seen the news in the last 24 hours. We hoped she'd warm to our cause but didn't expect anything.

"It's just up here, to the left" I said to Banjo as he was leading up front.

As we approached the house we saw Abby and her five foster kids playing out back on the swing.

"Get outa here you two dumb mother fuckers" she said to us.

This wasn't a wish for us to leave, more of a congratulatory statement.

"Wicked bruss, you two have got the whole town talking. The cops are fucking all over the joint looking for you man" said Abby with her hands waving in the air.

The kids stopped playing on the swing to see who we were.

"This is Uncle Banjo and Aunty Kirra. Say hello" said Abby.

"Hello" they all said at once.

There were five of them: Sally, Mick, David, Regina and Damien. They'd all been removed from various Aboriginal communities down south and placed with Abby in temporary care, which would almost certainly extend to permanent. Their families were in no position to look after them as glue and petrol sniffing had hit their communities hard. There is no way someone can take care of a child and sniff a can of petrol at the same time. The brain just can't handle that type of abuse I'm afraid. It never ends well, but what's important is that it doesn't end for the child. Sad fucking story I'm telling ya.

"What do you need? I've got some coffee and bread inside. Come in for a feed" said Abby.

She didn't have much to give, as she had mouths to feed, but what she had she was willing to share for a cause. The momentum was growing.

We went inside and pulled up a seat at the dining room table. Abby lived in a housing commission dwelling as we did on our community. The homes were basic in design and less than 100 square meters inside, so living was tight. With five kids and only three bedrooms she'd crammed them in the best she could, but they were safe with her and getting regular food, water, clothing and...love. They'd be ok but they needed to start going to school or the cycle would take its course and, well, we know the statistics.

Abby served coffee and toast and asked how Aunty Diane was.

"How is she man? I haven't seen her for ages. Is she still on the dialysis?" asked Abby.

I nodded. Aunty Diane had been a heavy drinker for many years and paid the price in her late 50s when she was diagnosed with kidney disease. She first noticed her yellow eyes in the mirror (Jaundice) when she was 45, then went to the doctor. It's a pretty terrible condition; death is slow and very painful. My heart bleeds for Aunty Diane.

"I'll be back soon, just need to get some air" said Banjo.

I and Abby were in deep conversation at the time so we didn't think much of it. Blokes need their own time I guess. He didn't return for about 20 minutes and I started to wonder where her was.

"Here ya go kids, fish and chips" said Banjo as he walked back in the door.

The kids jumped out of their seats and ran around the table three times. There was enough for everyone but we let the kids eat first.

"Look Nan, fisha! Chipa!" said Mick.

"Big chippy wa!!!!" said David.

"Banjo buddy!" said Regina.

"Champion bro" said Abby.

She would have added a swear word at the beginning but she tried not to swear around the kids. Everyone was happy, including Banjo who used his last $30 to pay for it all. The truth is, he loved kids as he was an only child. After his Dad died he lived with relatives who had kids but it wasn't the same as having brothers and sisters.

Banjo sat there, ate a few chips and laughed with the kids. It was his time to feel good and spread the wealth. If he had money, we all had money. That was the black fella way.

"So how long do you think you can both run for?" Said Abby with her hand over her mouth.

"Who knows, when it ends it ends" I said with puckered lips. "But I mean, it sounds like you have a plan. What's the next step?" Asked Abby.

"You could do what the others have done?" I asked.

"What the others have done? I hear they charged Jimmy for his part. He's out on bail" said Abby.

I looked at Banjo as he shook his head. This meant they'd charge Aunty Nat as well. Fuck it, I thought, they can't charge all of us.

"I'm ok with it actually. I mean someone needs to take a stand at some stage. It's been the same since I was their age" said Abby referring to the kids around the table. "I'm in bro, what do you need".

I had already written the statistics for her and placed them on the table. If all went to plan, there would be a double spread in tomorrow's paper with Aunty Nat and Abby on the front page.

Abby picked up the paper and read it out loud:

Indigenous children are almost 10 times more likely to be placed in out of home care than non-Indigenous children.

Indigenous households are more than 6 times as likely as other households to live in government housing commission.

20% of four to five-year olds are not attending preschool.

"Man, where do you get this stuff from?" Asked Abby.

"Books at school. They taught us this at high school. Don't you remember?" I asked.

Abby laughed. She got expelled for smoking Ganga (marijuana) in year 11. She was stoned pretty much from year 10 onwards. It's how she dealt with reality at the time.

We all cope somehow.

The stats were powerful enough to turn goat piss into gasoline, water to wine or perhaps a nation's attitude from apathy to a common interest. If this didn't happen, at the very least, the issues would come to light for all to see. Perhaps for a day, two days or a week? God build the world in seven days, so I guess it didn't have to be forever. It was a start I guess. Nobody ever finished anything without starting first.

Banjo looked at me with impatience then glanced at the door. He wanted to keep moving in case we had to fight yet another cop on the front lawn. This time they'd be better prepared I reckon. The next time they'd bring back up, perhaps a detective or alike. The situation was getting serious for the authorities who wanted a bust, and fast. The more times the news posted our faces and stats, the more embarrassment the government faced. It's the politicians that run the country here. The police are supposed to be a separate entity, but no way man. These red neck small country cities are like the south of Texas, where cowboy boots clip clop over all that exists, even the cops.

We said our goodbyes to Abby and the kids then slipped out the back door. The kids made a hell of a racket saying their goodbyes which was kind of cute. They're only kids so we didn't hush them down or rush out of sight. I reckon if anyone was near the house they could've planned an ambush right then and there, and that's exactly what happened. After five minutes of discussing our next move behind the back shed, I heard a sound at the front door. There were no cop cars, no sirens or cadets, just the noise of someone talking to Abby then the sound of a revolver clicking into firing position behind us.

"Police. Don't move" he said.

We did as instructed. We had no weapons so we could have just ran, he wouldn't have gone through with it. We were sure, but not that sure. He was a detective and his partner in crime had entered the front door just as we were leaving. Abby was inside locked in the toilet sending a text to the media with the story and stats. He threatened to break the door in, scaring the kids in the process. She got her message through so the story would make the papers the next morning. We could hear all this happening from behind the garden shed. I felt for the kids.

"Ok so what now you fucking hero. I'm unarmed, so is she. How about you put that gun down to even things up bruss, let's see how tough you are white fella" said Banjo.

His brain was beginning to shut down as it had before so I took him by the hand and whispered in his ear.

"Let's just go babe. It'll be ok" I whispered.

"No bruss, we can't stop now. We need to keep going, let's fight" he replied.

The detective tilted his head and cracked his neck, ready to shoot if he had to. I led Banjo to an unmarked cop car after tugging three times for him to move. His eyes were fixated on the cop and the challenge that was presented to him. They were doing the whole monkey see my chest thing that gets males into so much trouble. If only one would back down and walk away. But that never happens.

The cop handcuffed Banjo then put us both in the back seat. The media were just arriving so the cops wanted to leave quickly. The media guys were circling the suburb waiting for contact to be made so they were never far away. This was the biggest story for a year, perhaps in a decade as nothing much really happens here.

The cops battled with the camera man before giving up and getting into the car. We showed our faces as much as we could, and saw Abby give out the statistic. It was fucking magic.

"Hey!!, wooo!!, hey man over here" said Banjo as the camera turned their way.

"Hi Aunty Di and Nat, I love you!!" I said.

Banjo turned and looked at me.

I never said that. I mean, I feel it and show it but I never say it. Was this the first time? I didn't know why.

We waved goodbye to everyone getting some great coverage. The cops would surely try to stop it coming on the news tonight and in the newspapers the next day. The media is owned my Murdoch newspapers up here. This bloke had his own laws so we weren't worried. The Darwin guys wouldn't dare fuck with him for long.

Euphoria soon turned to dismay as the media disappeared into the distance and the sound of the cop radio blared into our ears. They were talking to the superintendent who was congratulating them on a job well done.

They were talking in code language which made us listen even harder, trying to decipher meaning so as to evaluate our situation. Whatever they were saying it didn't sound good. The only thing we had going for us at this stage was that two stats had been released and the media were still on our side. We were going to jail and we knew it, but we didn't flinch nor cry for mercy. We had done the best we could and gotten further than we thought. Was it over? We'd know in the next few hours at the cop station.

Chapter Five

We arrived at the Charles Darwin Police Station amidst a flurry of media and cop cars. There were lights flashing, blue uniforms and cameras everywhere. The flash photography almost blinded us as we drove slowly past all that awaited, then into a side entrance. The driver got out and opened our door. It was detective senior sergeant Alan Edwards. He was a bad ass cop who got results. I say bad ass because he was good at his job, although I wouldn't say that out loud. He had a fat guts and a grey beard that looked like colonel sanders. He just stood there and pulled his pants up, a sign of authority and certain intimidation.

"Get out of the car, we need to talk" he said.

We slid along the seat and hopped out. He led us to a holding cell that looked like a dorm of some sort, but it was secure. It was rectangular in shape with barred windows on each side with an adjoining courtyard that led to an open grass lawn. It was secured by a 12m fence with razor sharp barbed wire on top. No chance for an escape here.

It was tradition to leave suspects waiting in a cell before questioning to make them sweat a little. Sometimes detectives made people wait for several hours before they talked to them. The room had a TV, comfortable beds and a bar fridge with nothing in it. I wondered if this was an attempt at bad humour, especially as it had a VB sticker on the front.

I sat on the bed and watched some TV while Banjo went outside. He walked around the fence line and stared at the barb wire. His gaze never left the prickly steel as he walked with his head tilted upwards, stumbling on the odd occasion on a rock or grass root. The fence was a line drawn in the sand by the authorities. It would've been better if it was a wall of some sort, not a fence. He continued to pace back and forth like a caged animal then began to rub the back of his neck and roll his shoulders. He needed me.

I ran over and put my arms around his waist from behind. He stopped and looked down at the grass. I had broken his concentration - objective met.

"Come back inside babe, don't work yourself up" I said.

"How can you be so calm at a time like this? We've lost everything and we're in here. Aren't you pissed off at the world?" asked Banjo.

I guess I was, but I didn't want to show it in front of the cops who were watching us on CCTV. This was their technique to get some kind of confession and conviction. Watch, study and pounce. It was a mind game that Banjo wasn't capable of winning, so he needed my help, big time!

"Come inside and watch some TV" I said.

"Not Seinfeld for fuck sake, please?" said Banjo.

I knew my hug had worked by this stage. When Banjo calms he says something funny or nods a lot. I knew him well. We sat in bed and turned on the TV. I flicked through the channels for a while until the news came on. We were big news, really big. Up until that point I didn't know how big we were. The whole story had gone national with CNN also doing a cover story in the states. Our pictures and the heartbreaking stories of Nat, Jimmy and Abby's kids were shown on prime-time television. CNN were on their way to Darwin to try and get an interview with the authorities and perhaps us as well, although that would be unlikely in our current position.

"Look at the Kids bruss, and Jimmy, fucking hell man!" said Banjo laughing at the same time.

I couldn't say a word. I just sat there with a half-smile and tears in my eyes.

Community awareness was the ultimate goal. I didn't really know what to do next or could do really. Our actions had been classed as illegal by the authorities and I felt guilty about that, but how else do you start to change something that no one else wants to know about? News articles come and go and TV crews have their own agenda, so I knew the dust would settle and everything would go back to normal. I was in the clink with Banjo and our hands were tied for now. The cops wouldn't do anything for the time being until all this had blown over. We had to get out of there and continue what we started, and fast!

The cops quickly worked out that we'd got an emotional hit from the coverage so they pulled the TV plug from the outside. The news story had finished so we didn't care, although I wondered why they let us watch it in the first place.

"That's weird babe, did you see that" I asked Banjo.

"Yeah, I knew that would happen, fucking..." said Banjo before I cut him off.

"No, they let us watch the news coverage. Why man? That's fucked up" I said.

"They're fucked up" said Banjo.

I wasn't sure. Was this another tactic by the cops to screw with our minds? Happy one moment then depressed the next?

"Something about that detective Edwards. He's different to the other cops" I said.

"Yeah, the others are foot soldiers and he's the commandant" replied Banjo.

I scratched the back if my head and looked down at the tiled floor. I had a good feeling about the whole thing, just like I felt back at Mirambeena resort after me and Banjo had sex and were resting on the same pillow. I felt at ease, like everything would turn out ok in the end. I couldn't explain it. Weird man, really fucking weird.

We took another walk on the lawn area as there was nothing to do inside, as I wasn't having sex with a CCTV camera on us 24/7. We walked on the grass and felt the rough blades slide between our toes. We held hands and swayed our arms to and fro like lovers walking alongside a pond watching the ducks. It was a scene from a Jane Austin novel with our imaginations helping along the way. We were doing ok, but mainly because we had each other. If Banjo was alone it would be a different story.

We heard the door to our room open. We were at the back fence at the time so we just stood there and waited for a cop to come out. The guard removed something from the room and left.

"What the fuck was that?" Asked Banjo.

"Dinner time maybe, let's check it out" I said.

We walked back into the room and looked around. We didn't realise what they'd taken right away but eventually noticed the bedsheets were gone.

"They took the fucking sheets. Do they think this will stop us from sleeping or something?" Asked Banjo.

"I dunno, let's ask them" I said.

Banjo knocked on the door.

"Hey, what the fuck was that? Why did you take the sheets man, give em back" said Banjo.

We could hear a muffled voice from behind the door; something about safety or alike. Banjo froze then lifted his head and stared at the ceiling. He looked angry again. I took his hand. It was cold, really cold. He was starting to shut down.

"Give them back you bastards! What do you think I am man? Give them back!" said Banjo.

The memories of his father began to flow back into the present. His traumatic past began to haunt him once again with images of his father hanging himself in a cell using a bed sheet. This was a common way to end it all when us black fellas struggled with a sudden loss of freedom without understanding why.

"Banjo, let's sit down, c'mon its ok. Turn the TV back on please" I asked.

There was no response.

"Banjo, let's go, back out to the grass. Let's go man" I said. It was no use. His brain had shut down with the effects of trauma about to surface, like a sea serpent ready to strike.

Banjo began to slam his fist against the door.

"You fuckers man! Give the sheets back! Give me my Dad back" he shouted.

He continued to punch the door.

"Give them back to me. Give him back to me, you fuckers, you mother fucking fuckers!!"

He began to cry.

"Give my Dad back to me!!" he shouted.

"Give my Dad back to me!" he said.

The pounding of his fist began to weaken as he dropped to his knees.

"Give him back to me" he whispered.

He collapsed onto the floor.

"I want my Dad back" he thought to himself.

I stood there crying, holding my hands to my face. He'd completely shut down at this point and had probably broken his fist as well. I waited for someone to come in and help but that never happened. I didn't care. I could handle this.

"Babe, Banjo get up man. Don't worry man, I'm here for you.

Come with me" I said.

He got up and walked on his hands and knees to the bed and collapsed with his head on my lap. I ran my fingers through his hair and told him that everything would be ok. This was all he could understand at this point in the aftermath of a severe trauma attack. When you see the violence in communities, the car park brawls, and the substance abuse, it's all connected to trauma in some way. It's not that we black fellas are bad, we've just had evil shit done to us. What goes in must come out, usually in dribs and drabs from the depths of hell!

We both curled up and fell asleep in each other's arms. I woke up a few times during the night and walked the perimeter fence to try and think of our next move. The cops were using the 'wait and see' technique, so we'd be here for a few more hours before anything happened. I knew that Banjo couldn't handle this place for long. He'd do something stupid for sure.

It was 3am when I awoke again to a rattling sound. I went outside and scanned the perimeter. When I got to the far end gate I noticed the padlock was gone. It was there before, my oath it was. This was a detention lockup so all locks were present and checked twice a day. The lock had been removed. Someone was helping us. We had a secret admirer in the shadows of society, a Father Christmas in disguise perhaps. This was evidence of mass community support for the issues at hand. It was a sign to continue our good work which was far from done.

I went back into the room and shook Banjo.

"Babe, babe wake up man, we're out of here" I said.

"What, outa here? Did we make bail?" Asked Banjo.

"Not likely. The gate to the far side is open. Someone unlocked it babe" I said.

He lifted his head, roughed up his hair with one hand then looked around. He was still recovering from a massive trauma attack, but he could now speak ok.

"Where? Show me where" he said.

I led him to the gate in the corner. It was a small single gate with a bolt going across minus the padlock.

"Let's go then, c'mon" said Banjo.

I hesitated for a second. I don't know why. Why does one hesitate? Out of fear I guess. Fear of the failure? Fear of success? Fear of the unknown? I needed to move, even one step would do. Banjo grabbed me by the hand and opened the gate softy, then pulled me through; much like he did at the gap in the fence at Woolworths. I had given him the strength to carry on. He'd taken it the rest of the way. We were fucking magic together.

"This way, let's go" said Banjo.

"No fucking way man, that leads to the front door. Do you want to go back in again?" I asked.

He didn't respond.

"This way, into the scrub" I said.

"What the fuck, its 5km to the next road that way, are you mad woman?" He asked.

"Yes I'm a woman but no I'm not mad. Who just brought you back from the dead and looked after you babe? Me, that's who. Now this way" I said.

"Man, what a woman" he said with a smile.

A cheesy one liner but I liked it.

We walked for five minutes through the thick scrub and were already regretting it. There were spiders, big sand flies that ate human flesh and mosquitoes that carried Ross river virus - a type of Malaria. We didn't have a compass or anything to guide the way but we knew the road was in a straight line from the lockup.

"Fucking Jesus, I can't handle this babe. The fucking mozzies are killing me. We've got to get to the swamp over yonder" said Banjo.

"That's where they live. We'll be going into their home, won't we?" I asked.

"No that's where the sand flies live" replied Banjo.

"Sand flies live in the mud? So why don't they call them mud flies?" I asked.

He didn't reply.

With all the small talk happening we didn't notice the distance we'd travelled. We were about half way to the road when we came across a small river. We covered ourselves with mud from head to toe to deter the mozzies, then pressed on. It was the wet season so we didn't hang around in the water for long, as the crocodiles could be anywhere at this time of year.

"Look out for bubbles babe. Did you see any?" Asked Banjo.

"The water isn't deep so I didn't look" I replied.

We then saw a two-metre croc surface only metres from where we were standing. It could have lunged at any time but it didn't.

"Perhaps the croc is helping us somehow? We have a secret croc angel" I said.

Banjo laughed as he continued to make a path through the bushes, kicking them with his feet and pulling down creeper vine with his bare hands. I was impressed, as any girl would be.

"Shhhh! Can you hear that?" I asked.

"What? No nothing" replied Banjo.

"There again, people talking. It's an Aboriginal dialect. Let's check it out" I said.

We turned on a right angle and walked for 30 metres until we came across a 'long grass' shanty town. We saw a group of fringe dwellers that had it much worse than us. Much worse than anyone. They were homeless of course and made their homes from cardboard or scrap sheet metal of some kind. There were filthy mattresses laying on the ground covered in mud with dirty blankets thrown on top. They endured the mozzies and the sand flies, but these were the least of their problems. They often had domestic disputes which were extremely violent, causing injuries that were never treated. They spoke little English so they couldn't cry for help or make a statement to the police if needed, they had no phone to call for help and knew only themselves as friends. They had hearing loss with constant puss coming from their ear canals, filthy hair, STDs, rotten teeth, scabies, Jaundice, cut feet and were hungry with no access to fresh water. They were isolated like a pigmy tribe in remote Africa, and were perhaps the most vulnerable humans alive, even though they were only five minutes from the largest police station in metro Darwin.

"Man, can you believe this shit babe?" Banjo asked from the bushes.

"I thought we had it hard, fuck me!" I said.

"We need to help them, let's go?" said Banjo.

"What do you think we are doing? Spreading the word is how we can help the most" I said.

"We need to help where we can, every chance counts babe" replied Banjo.

"Are all these people sticking up for us for nothing? There all getting charged. Even Aunty Nat and she might lose her teacher registration. We need to think big, let's go" I said.

I peeled Banjo from the scene and we pressed on. It would take a community effort to fix all these problems. I needed to think of a way to rally all this support and to come together with a unified approach. I had the drive but not the knowhow. The answer would come. We just needed to band together.

Dawn broke from the heavens as we neared the main road. We were covered in mud from head to toe but still had mozzie bites on our backs and arms. They are persistent little suckers and never give up, no matter how well covered you are.

We looked like army veterans from the Vietnam War after escaping the Viet Kong or something. Or perhaps we could have passed as long grasses, but that wasn't funny. We would come back for them or think of something. We had their backs, they just didn't know it.

As we stumbled onto the road in the morning light we could see a road block in the faint distance. The cops would go to any lengths possible to get us back, and we would do the same to fulfil our destinies. Easy words for a couple of teenagers with nowhere to go but back into the scrub. We trusted our instincts implicitly, so much so that we waved down the next car that passed by.

Banjo whistled as a Holden Utility dove by at half the speed limit. They were expecting a relative of sort or perhaps a family friend.

She stopped and wound down the window.

"Everyone's looking for you two. What's the story?" She said. "Story? Were just trying to help that's all" I said.

Her name was Sarah, a correctional officer at the local juvenile detention centre next to the police station. She'd worked with Aboriginal youth for years and knew the issues they were tackling. She was a white girl with a stocky build. She didn't wear makeup to work and dressed in overalls each day as she liked the hands-on stuff, like gardening and me-chanics.

They didn't have much time. It was either get in and go or be noticed by the cops.

"Get in the back, they'll wave me on at the block. Hurry up" said Sarah.

They looked at each other and jumped in the back.

"Pull the tarp over" said Sarah.

They did everything they were asked. What choice did they have?

The road block was diverted into two streams on arrival as they couldn't stop everyone. We entered the left-hand stream and were promptly waved on. Sarah gave the officer in charge a wave and smile as she took a left turn to the 'Dan Gale' Ju-venile detention centre. We cringed in the back, trying to hear what we could. It was hot, really hot and we hoped to reach our destination soon.

Banjo gestured to me with his hands wide open and a confused look upon his face.

"Why did we do this?" He whispered.

"No choice buddy. It was either this or back to the swamp with cops and crocs all over the place" I replied quietly.

"She's taking us to Dan Gale. That's a fucking juvenile detention centre. We're juveniles man!!" said Banjo.

"Trust the process bro and chill" I replied.

He covered his face and shut down again.

They entered via the back entrance of the centre and parked in shade, then Sarah peeled the tarp off the back off her Ute.

"Are you fried lizards yet?" Asked Sarah.

We didn't know what to say or how to respond. Was she referring to the heat in the back or what lay ahead for us inside? We were about to run.

"Don't panic. I want you two inside as guests. I'm really proud that someone has finally taken a stand on some of these horrendous issues and got some results. Come inside and we'll talk" said Sarah.

She looked nice so we went with her. Anyway, we wanted to get inside to meet the kids that were locked up and ask some questions. This would be a good place to release a new statistic and continue our dream run of media coverage. This was magic man; so many people willing to help in such a short space in time. It felt to me, that everyone was just waiting in keep until someone took a stand; existing in their own personal space until activated. Leadership can come from anywhere, even a 17-year-old girl from Kiranya.

Chapter Six

We entered Dan Gale from a side entrance like guest speakers to a conference. Sarah's office was away from the general population so we stayed in there until we had a chance to talk.

"What can we do here?" Asked Banjo.

"You tell me, you're the crusaders with all the support. What can you do?" Said Sarah.

"Can we go in and talk to everyone? I'd like to hear about what goes on here" I asked.

Sarah bit her lip. She didn't expect me to ask that. I think they had something to hide. She looked at me with her hand on her mouth then looked down at the ground. She had something important to say.

"I guess when I first saw you two on the road I was hesitant to pick you up. I just thought you needed some help. When I saw who you were I knew you could turn our situation around. I'll be honest with you, things aren't great here. 60% of our cohort are Aboriginal and we are not getting the results we want. Perhaps you can shed some light on the place? If you can make some good suggestions, I'll post one of your statistics" she said.

"You'll get the sack. They'll never let you stay here if you do that" said Banjo.

"True, but to be a part of what you've stated is a lot more important than my job. I'll find another one" said Sarah. I almost cried. Here was a white girl willing to sacrifice her livelihood for a cause. I say A cause now, not MY cause. To transfer ownership over to the community would be the ultimate goal.

"Are you sure?" I asked.

"Sure I'm sure, if you're friends can take a hit and be charged for aiding a criminal then we all need to put ourselves out there. Not everyone will do it but if enough participate then the authorities will fold. You can't expel every kid in the school to maintain order. One is made an example of, perhaps two, then after that the Principal needs to come up with something else. I am right?" Asked Sarah.

Both I and Banjo nodded.

"Ok what I'll do is introduce you as new inmates for the day and you can have free reign. Find out what you need to make your point and I'll share the statistic like the others" said Sarah.

I looked at Banjo with disbelief. He looked at me and smiled.

We looked at Sarah and said "no problem".

We'd heard a lot about this place but was unsure what was fact from fiction. We would find out soon enough.

"Banjo, the guard down the hall will take you to the men's block and Kirra, I'll take you to the female wing. You've got 3 hours. If you get into any trouble let the guard know you want to speak to me" said Sarah.

This was a gold mine. Man, no one is allowed access to this place, unless you've been locked up of course. I've heard some pretty evil shit goes down here, but it's all here say, no one can prove anything unless there's inside info coming out.

Enter me and Banjo onto the scene. We'd shine a torch on this shit and kick up the dust. I was excited. I was making progress. I was Kirra Yunupingu.

By the time I'd entered general population everyone knew I was coming. Word of mouth travels quicker than a speeding bullet, especially when people are excited because change is in the air. I didn't have to introduce myself to anyone and no one said hello. It's not customary to make a big deal in the lock up when someone special arrives. The best greeting that anyone gets is a golf clap using only the palms to soften the impact. This is usually used at adult prisons but sometimes happens in youth detention centres. I didn't get one, but that's ok. That's not why I was there.

I sat at the mess table eating bangers and mash, looking around at the many faces of incarceration. 60% of them were Aboriginal, taking into account that we only make up 3% of the entire Australian population. They looked sombre even though the food tasted good. It seems incidental, but good food can ease the mind at the worst of times. If the food was shit and the company was shit, it made for a pretty shitty life. At least one aspect of their lives was worth looking forward to, even though it only lasted for ten minutes or so.

The sound of knives scraping, cups landing on the bench and the many darting looks to each side dominated proceedings. The sights and sounds all mixed together to form an opinion of one another and what lay ahead the next session. Although everyone looked comfortable and ready to kick back on a Sunday morning, there was always something else on their mind; who wanted to get them, who they wanted to get, what happened yesterday, what they could get from the outside and... how the fuck do we get out of this chicken shit outfit? All these thoughts going in and out of the mind nurtured by bangers and mash and fresh milk packed neatly into a small carton. It was subdued chaos at best, as just beneath the surface lay a world of hurt and anguish, and when their plate was clean and milk carton empty, it was then time to act on those thoughts that presented themselves in a moment of solitude and safety.

I finished my meal and walked over to the kitchen to hand over my plate. There were three girls standing there as they'd finished first, which meant they'd eaten first. They were tall, well-groomed and obviously friends. The tallest one was standing in the middle. She was the leader and had positioned herself nicely at the top end of the pecking order. This meant privileges inside: more food, high status, more friends and above all…leadership status. If there were issue then it would be discussed with her first. If someone wanted to crack a skull, she would be the first to know.

Her name was Bindi. She was removed at an early age as her parents were long grasses and didn't take her to school. They said she could learn from nature but the government didn't see it that way. At an imposing 6 feet 3 inches tall with a wiry build and new Adidas sneakers, she commanded respect. If she didn't get it, she'd hit you so fucking damn hard that you'd change your mind about the situation, and quickly. Brute force was her backup plan, or if she just wanted to get you, it was the only one.

She turned around and looked at me, followed by the other two who copied her every move.

"You're that Kirra girl from Kiranya mob" she said.

It was not a question.

The other two girls looked at Bindi then back at me.

"Yeah bud, that's right. Are we cool?" I asked.

"Are we cool, well let's see? You appear out of nowhere, stand behind me waiting, stare at everyone at the table, don't say hello and pay your respects, ask me a question on your first day and then call be Bud. Let's fucking think about that hmmm….no, we're not ok" replied Bindi.

I felt shit loosening in my bowels ready to drop on the floor. I held my ass tight for a few seconds until I regained my composure. I wasn't going to let this girl get the better of me. Perhaps it was a test of some sort? Or perhaps she woke up grumpy and yearned for some modified shadow boxing after breakfast? Who fucking knows, but I was on their turf and had to adhere to the culture.

I was only one person among many and wasn't that special.

Just because I'd started a revolution it didn't mean shit in the inside unless you paid respect and followed the rules, at least initially.

"Full respect Aunty Bindi" I said.

By calling her Aunty it showed both subservient behaviour and respect. It was the highest honour that an elder female could receive. It nearly always melted hearts and was common place right across Australia.

Bindi stared me down whilst the other two waited for their instructions. She looked at my shirt, then at my face, then into my eyes. It was here that she saw strength and self-respect built on past experience. She saw humility and self-determination in an environment that served no other purpose but to punish and detain.

Bindi stared me down for a few seconds longer. By this time, her two off siders were getting nervous, very nervous. Was this girl to take one of their places? Would Bindi ask them to do a job on her? They waited in the abyss of silence.

"Fuck off you two. Go make my bed" said Bindi to her offsiders.

They left with their eyes rolling. Perhaps if they'd shown the same level of strength as I did then things would've been different. Servants are always replaceable.

"I'm inviting you to my cell" said Bindi.

I lowered my head to accept her invitation. We walked together past the others who were still eating. This was all that was required to let everyone know that I was now accepted. If anyone had a beef with me, they needed to talk it over with Bindi first. Even though I was only there for a few hours and some kind of celebrity in the community, the rules stuck and culture still applied. I was no exception, only the top dog was, and there were always challenges.

"Thanks Aunty" I said to Bindi as we walked alongside the jail cells.

I had decided to only call her Aunty for the remainder of my stay. This had already started to work as she smiled and showed me around the centre.

"This is medium and low security where we can walk around after school. Some of us choose to work out but the majority just hang out" said Bindi.

"What happens at hang out time?" I asked.

"We talk, gossip and fight usually" she replied.

"But there's other things to do Aunty, look a games room and TV" I said.

"Don't fucking patronise me mother fucker. We hang out, gossip and fight. It doesn't matter what's around at the time.

That's what we do" she said.

"Yes Aunty" I replied.

Fair enough I thought. I hadn't been to the lock up so what the fuck did I know. I think that's what she was trying to tell me.

We didn't have access to maximum security. That's where Bindi was placed in her first month at Dan Gale, and that's where all the shit happens. You don't go into that wing unless you've got some serious fucking issues, which means you get some serious fucking help and intervention right? No fucking way bruss. If you go in there you're like a shit in a PIT toilet rotting on the bottom of a hole dug in the ground. The smell never goes away as there's no flushing system, and neither do the issues.

Bindi pointed to maximum security through a barred window. "There it is, one step away from the big house we are. The place smells like shit" she said.

"You've got to get me in there man. Can you wave your wand and get me inside?" I asked.

"What for? What are you up to?" Asked Bindi.

She began to distrust me. I needed to come clean.

"Ok I'm only here for a few hours, Sarah let me in from the outside" I said.

"You're still fucking at large and you volunteered to come here? What the fuck is wrong with you bruss? This is where you come when it's all over. Here's my cell, get in here" said Bindi. "Tell me everything or I'll split your head open like a watermelon" exclaimed Bindi.

I didn't buy it. She wasn't violent. I could see in her eyes that she'd had a bad upbringing and all that, but she wouldn't do anything like that. I just sat and smiled back.

Bad move bruss.

She grabbed me, pulled my hair back and placed me in the windpipe pincer grip, like Darth Vader when he choked someone to death with the force. Bindi wasn't quite that powerful so she used her hand. I couldn't breathe, obviously. Her grip tightened around my throat as oxygen gathered around my nostrils, begging to enter.

She moved closer to my face.

"If you don't do everything I tell you to do, when I tell you to and how I tell you to do it, then I'll rip your throat out" She said to me.

She slammed my head against the mattress which was soft and comfortable so I didn't mind. I was way out of my depth in terms of muscle power. I'd slipped up and become complacent in an environment where violence and mob brutality overrides intellectual prowess. The law of the fist reigns supreme here. Step out of line and you find out who's boss. She had it over me from this point. I thought I'd seen the face of God.

I got up and sat on the bed.

"Fuck man I'm sorry Aunty. You got me man, anything you say" I said.

What choice did I have? Sarah wasn't there to jump in and save the day. I had to conform.

"Tell me everything Kiranya girl, and I mean… fucking… everything!" Said Bindi with her finger pointed at my head.

"Ok, Sarah let us in for a few hours to get some dirt. I can then bump out one of my stats and she calls the media and police to DOB us in. The cops come running and the media publish another article in the news. We've got CNN in the mix here as well" I said.

"Why not just wait in the car park and do it all from there. Why risk your life and come in here?" Asked Bindi.

"The cops will ask everyone inside to verify the truth. People will make statements and CCTV footage will be released" I said.

"Yeah, I read all this in the newspaper, but I wasn't sure about it all. Hmmm, ok, so you're a crusader eh?" she said.

"I'm getting results man, and that's all that matters" I said. She stared me down yet again to see if I was telling the truth. Bindi hated people lying to her. It's probably the number one thing that set her off. It was rejection you see. Anything that even remotely resembled rejection caused an outbreak of trauma related violence. It was all her interpretation; being lied to, not getting her way, people talking about her. Man, what a fucking nightmare. The child psychiatrists need to get in here and help, but there are only two of them in the entire state and they don't come to places like this. There are physiologists yeah, but most of them don't know what the fuck their doing, usually young graduates who form close relationships with the kids but nothing more. Their more like social workers than anything else. The kids here don't need another friend, they need help, serious fucking help.

"You do realise all the shit in here has already been published in the royal commission they did?" Said Bindi.

"Yeah, I know, has anything changed?" I asked.

"Only the use of tear gas, restraint chairs and solitary confinement. But that's all over in maximum security, but I reckon they still use the chairs" said Bindi.

The chairs were used for ages in the prison. They had straps on the arms and a back rest. If an inmate had an episode, he or she would be placed in the chair with a bag over their heads until they calmed. Really bad shit man I can tell ya. Most western countries got rid of those years ago, actually many years ago.

"I've been in one" said Bindi.

"How long for?" I asked.

"Fucking long enough. The first five minutes are the worst. It was my second week here and I'd punched out two guards at the same time. They dragged me down the hall by my hair like an animal. I yelled, kicked and screamed as they put me in the chair. It took three people and a whole lotta power. They put a bag over my head and tightened the rope around my throat.

That was the killer. That felt like being hanged, like a feral back fella in the bush. Like a black cotton plantation girl being hung for dropping a dozen eggs. I felt like an animal. I didn't understand how they thought it would make me any better. How it would have improved the situation. I was fucked up by my parents when I was young and this was the cure? I don't understand it, I just don't fucking get it man, I really don't. Fuck" she said.

Her two friends had heard the commotion and were standing outside the cell. Firstly, they thought that I'd done something to her and wanted my head. They saw Bindi cry for the first time and didn't know what to do. Just a few tears came that day, but it was more than she'd cried in months. It was a way to release the hurt, at least I thought so.

She'd gone from searing anger to despair within three minutes, from one extreme to the other. Life's a type rope man, I'm telling ya.

I stayed there sitting on the end of the bed until she'd composed herself. By this time her friends had gone elsewhere, thinking that our conversation was private. She kept wiping the tears from her eyes, but others soon replaced them. Bindi disguised this beautifully by a constant wiping motion that looked like she was waking up on a cold morning. To cry showed weakness, especially with a stranger in the room.

"Ok" I said as I moved over and laid on her bed "it's ok to cry. Let it out man"

"Get off my fucking bed!" was her response.

She didn't say this with anger, it was more like a whimper to hide the fact that she was upset. Bindi was an expert at hiding pain, but the more it stayed in the darkness with the mothballs and dust, the more it grew mould, becoming infectious and causing disease. Her sickness was trauma and it was as common as the flu in her neighbourhood.

We talked some more about the centre and what she liked about school.

"Fucking nothing, except the teacher of course. She's nice, always has been. I don't like anything else and I don't do any work. I just sit there and listen to her motherly tone and watch her short blonde hair bounce all over the place. If I had my time over I'd be like her. A school teacher I reckon" said Bindi.

"You're time over again, shit you're only 17 babe. Same age as me" I said,

"Yeah, and look how far you've come" she said.

"Aw fucking nice girl" I said jokingly.

We were making a connection. She had put on the bully girl act to perfection, but now I was seeing the real Bindi. It only took 30 minutes or so. I just wondered if she would ever see what I was looking at; a beautiful young lady with potential. If she'd just drop the violent babe in the woods routine she'd be on top of her game. I wanted to help her, I wanted to help those long grasses I saw, I wanted to save my community. Fuck, did I want too much? No way man, I was going for it, big time.

"Hey Sarah, where have you been?" said Bindi looking over my shoulder.

"Paperwork my dear. How are you travelling?" She asked.

"Fucked" replied Bindi.

"Better than yesterday then?" asked Sarah.

Yesterday she was really fucked. This was all an attempt at humour of course. I liked her.

"Any chance I can get you to counselling this time?" asked Sarah.

"No chance, zero.......who is it?" Asked Bindi.

"Catherine" replied Sarah.

"The lady with the dead straight hair and nice teeth?" asked Bindi.

"That's the one" said Sarah.

"Not interested, she's a phoney" said Bindi looking at her nails.

Sarah crossed her arms and walked out the door. Bindi had only been to three sessions in six months.

"Who do you like?" I asked.

"People who actually give a shit" she replied still looking at her nails.

"Me too" I said "me too".

I could see Sarah across the hall talking to three other inmates. They were looking at me with much interest so I decided to go over and introduce myself.

"Will I see you again?" I asked Bindi.

"Only if you end up in here I guess. But you have other plans, right?" asked Bindi.

"Other than getting caught you mean?" I replied jokingly. I tapped on the bars lightly and left her alone. She'd be alright.

When I reached the cells opposite, Sarah asked us all to come into her office at the end of the hall. She had a working air conditioner and coke in the fridge which she only gave out on special occasions. She gave me a coke then asked the other three kids. One said yes and the others declined. They all looked nervous.

"Kirra, these are the tear gas victims. This is Tania, Alice and Sam. They all looked at her and nodded. They knew who she was and I knew who they were. About six months ago they were tear gassed by staff who accused them of rioting in the prison even though CCTV footage showed only one of them banging on the door. No one outside the royal commission had seen this footage until now, even the girls, se we were about to be part of a privileged few. Sarah played the tape as we all sat back looking up at the wall mounted TV. The CCTV vision showed the girls reactions as they were affected by the gas, running to the back of their cells, hiding behind sheets and mattresses, gasping for air, crying, and bending over toilets. Alice was left in her cell and exposed to tear gas for ten minutes. She laid face down on the floor with her hands behind her back, before being handcuffed by two prison officers wearing gas masks, then dragged out of her cell. Before the gassing, they were kept locked in their cells for almost 72 hours straight with no running water, little natural light, and denied access to school and educational material.

Tania broke down immediately. She wiped the corner of her eyes a few times then began to cry uncontrollably. She crossed her arms as tight as she could to block out the pain, then looked up at the ceiling for guidance. Only the white paint that peeled in even cracked rows offered relief in the form of a much-needed distraction.

"I shouldn't have watched that. Fucking Jesus man" Tania said still with tears flowing from her eyes and onto the floor.

"Why did they do that Sarah? You were here what the fuck happened?" Asked Sam.

"The two guards made a decision. I wasn't there. But I'm here now, I'm here for you guys and to find a way forward" said Sarah.

Sarah was a qualified counsellor. She wanted to fix them all but was only allocated a set amount of kids. This session was a time to see the full version of the footage. It was a time to cry, hold hands and face the truth.

"Kirra, can you do something? Can you tell CNN to play the extended version worldwide?" asked Tania.

"I think they'll do that anyway. I haven't talked to them yet. I'm not sure I'll be able to" I replied.

"I'll talk to you about that later. I've got a plan" said Sarah. I looked at Sarah and wondered what the plan was. Like myself and Banjo, she was also a crusader; she wanted what we did but had a few more ideas on exactly how to create long lasting change. Interviews, media coverage and newspaper articles come and go, but new systems that are put in place have a much greater effect. I was the catalyst for change as the saying goes. I now needed a round table of healthy minds to put something into place.

"What now Sarah, what can we do?" asked Tania.

Sarah and I looked at each other and smiled. She knew why she was smiling but I didn't. I was just smiling because she was. I guess I trusted her, anyway I needed some help. After all, there was no point getting this far and everything just going back to normal in a few weeks. I think that's what everyone was expecting.

"Rest assured girls, your experience won't go to waste" said Sarah.

"So you're gonna get them then? You're going to get revenge for us?" asked Sam.

"Not quite. There's no point in that. We need to put something in place so your kids don't end up in here" replied Sarah.

All three girls laughed at the prospect of having kids. It was a laugh filled with excitement and trepidation as they were so young with so many questions about the future. What was important is that this never happened again and that something good came of it.

The girls looked closely at the two adults in the room. They'd been promised the world before and came up empty handed. They didn't trust anyone from an authoritative position as that type put them away to begin with. There was silence, a golden silence as the likelihood of trust was established with a series of darting glares, crossed arms, legs stretched out, a few deep breaths and a discerning stare, and then it was all over. The girls nodded and left the room. I didn't make any promises but it was kind of like I did. I had to follow through for them, for Aunty Nat, for Jimmy, for the long grasses, for Abby, for Banjo, and for me.

I walked with Sarah out the back entrance to maximum security where she pretended to be my escort. I had to hold my hands behind my back and look pissed off to get past the guards. They knew Sarah but they also knew something was up when they saw my face. No one had been notified of my arrival and that wasn't common practice.

"Fuck, those guards suspected something" I said to Sarah as we entered the main doors.

"I know, we don't have much time" replied Sarah.

She showed me the restraint chairs and the hood they used on Bindi and countless others. It looked like a KKK outfit for a black fella, if that makes sense, with the only difference being no holes for the eyes or a slit near the mouth to breath oxygen. I put it on and almost choked within 30 seconds. I could breathe, but only just. This was fucking torture man. The United Nations backed that up in their report to the government. They didn't listen.

"Hop in" said Sarah.

"What! I haven't done anything wrong" I said.

You'll get a better feel for the situation if you're in the driver's seat" said Sarah.

Could I trust her? Would you?

I looked at her face and saw a lady trying to make a point. She looked sincere but these authority types always turned on a coin and played the good cop bad cop routine to perfection.

"Fuck it" I said and sat down.

Sarah looked at my face and did up the straps. She could see the fear in my eyes as did Pennywise the evil clown as he approached his young victims in the sewer. Stephen King is the best man. I was relaxed because I knew it wasn't real. I just sat there and looked at her. Then came the hood and the rope used to tie it around my neck. It wasn't too tight but then again I couldn't breathe. Sarah turned off the light and left the room. I panicked and yelled out to her.

"Sarah get the fuck back in here!" I demanded.

There was no answer. I moved my whole body to try and loosen the straps then got a cramp in my left calf muscle but couldn't straighten my leg. It was fucking agony. My feet began to swell as did my throat. I couldn't yell out anymore as I was beginning to cry. I whimpered behind that hood praying for peace to return. It was fucking torture man, absolute fucking torture. I was really scared and close to breaking point and I'd only been there for three minutes. Bindi had to endure forty-five.

"Now you know what's it's like to be a prisoner in fear" said Sarah from behind me as she took off the hood.

I looked up and wanted to abuse the fuck out of her. I wanted revenge against authority. I wanted to crack her skull. Then I heard what she said again in my own head 'to live in fear'. What? Was I truly going to understand the situation by visiting a few inmates and asking questions then walk away with sympathy? I had to live it, and Sarah had provided the vehicle. I still wanted to crack her skull though. After 45 minutes I would have taken her life, scary shit man.

Sarah unstrapped me and stood at the door waiting. She didn't apologise nor did she need to. This was something I had to learn the hard way. I had learnt to live in fear as a prisoner.

"Fucking bitch" I said as I met her at the door.

She smiled.

I wasn't angry, just pissed off. I wouldn't seek revenge but I did kick her in the shin as I passed by. She smiled at me again.

I didn't respond.

If only I'd done this before I talked to Bindi and the three girls, perhaps I would've approached things differently? Or maybe I would have lost the plot and ran back out the door with Banjo.

"Shit, Banjo, where is he?" I asked.

"Relax he's in the boys wing doing the same thing as you?" replied Sarah as we walked back out the door to minimum security.

"I need to see him, I need to get out of here" I said.

I was really worked up from being in the chair. I found it really hard to breathe and I needed my freedom. If I'd been dragged back to a cell at that time I think I would have topped myself, and I wondered if anyone had. I needed to see the sky, to feel the fresh air coming across the ocean and eat an ice cream at the shops. I wanted my freedom. As shitty as my life was, at least I still had that.

Sarah put her arm around me as we walked back to her office. I was smiling at that time and secretly forgave her for teaching me a life lesson in fear and injustice.

"You'll feel better once we get back to my office. I've got a proposal for you" said Sarah.

This sounded exciting but I didn't show it. I could still feel the leather straps of that fucking chair on my wrists and was hesitant to receive any further lessons in humanity. I did trust her, I just felt a bit empty at the time.

"Banjo" I cried as I saw him down the hallway next to Sarah's office.

I ran and jumped on his back as he was talking to a guard. He spun around and ran up and down the hall with me like a wild bull. We stopped in front of Sarah and I dismounted. We were laughing.

"In you two, you're making a scene" said Sarah as she ushered us into her office.

I debriefed with Banjo about Bindi, the gassing incident and our visit to maximum security. I didn't tell him about the chair as I knew he'd react. With love comes a sense of obligation to protect. It's the most powerful emotion I know of. I was careful about what I told him. I had to be.

"So, what about you? Any news from the land of testosterone?" I asked Banjo.

"Well I saw Max and Danny from Bagot and Jimmy's brother who's in for possession. I passed by the ghost cell that everyone talks about then came back here" said Banjo.

"What ghost cell?" I asked.

"The 'Neddy' cell where that boy killed himself a while back. He was sentenced to 28 days detention under mandatory sentencing laws for stealing petrol and he got a lifetime" said Banjo.

"He was in no condition to be in that cell by himself. No one was watching him and he just said goodbye in his own way" said Sarah with a heavy heart.

There've been more suicides than that, but this one was the straw that broke Darwin's back. This one got into the papers and stirred some shit. I guess that's what I'm doing - stirring shit so the news can get their stories and the newspapers can have their headlines. That's what Sarah wanted to talk to us about.

We sat and looked at Sarah. She took a deep breath and looked at us with intention.

"You guys need help. You've come all this way and achieved so much, but without community engagement this will blow over in a month" said Sarah.

We hadn't actually thought about the future. We were just happy that Aboriginal injustices were in the spotlight, both nationally and internationally.

"Someone is waiting for you in the next room. Her name is Lauren Wilson. She's a senior CNN reporter from America. She wants your story to go worldwide. What do you say?" asked Sarah.

"So how will that gain community support?" I asked.

"Well, it will at least get you international support. We then hit hard locally and keep up the pressure" she said.

"Go on" I said.

"With you crusading the lands giving stats with the media as support, a few chosen community members can then rally everyone to form a movement" said Sarah.

I wasn't familiar with this type of strategy. I wasn't familiar with strategy at all. I was just a kid wanting to make a difference in this big bad world that shat on me whenever it had the chance. That's why I needed her help.

"Put it this way, you keep up the pressure and I will coordinate certain people to take action in the community.

There are a lot of souls out there just waiting to be led in the right direction. Most people know wrong from right, they just don't know what to do" said Sarah.

"Ok I think I understand. So where's this lady then? I want to meet her" I said.

I wanted to get going, to yet again ignite the activist inside me and light a fire under society and then…....? I guess this is why I needed Sarah's help. It all started to make sense.

Banjo opened the door for the American reporter like a gentleman.

"Good morning all, how are ya! Top morning isn't it? I'm Lauren, Lauren Wilson from the big apple. Glad to be here" she said.

I felt sick.

How could someone talk so fast and yet say so little? I wanted to leave.

Banjo nudged me as she sat down with her note book and pencil. She was a thin elderly lady with dark rimmed glasses and a smile that went from ear to ear. The wrinkles on her face spoke a thousand tales of years gone by which she didn't try to hide with anti-ageing cream or make up of any kind. She looked proud and wanted to be there.

"I am so, so existed to be here. Golly gosh I've never been to the land of Aus. before. I'm so passionate about Aboriginal issues and I wanna help" she said with her hands waving about in front of her face.

She had travelled thousands of miles to be here so we had to suck it up and work with her.

There was no time to mock indifferences or make fun of an accent. If we did that then what were we doing all this for? We had to set the example and pucker up.

"Great to see you, I've watched CNN a few times through the pub window. I couldn't hear the sound but the pictures looked interesting" I said.

"Yeah, how are ya miss?" said Banjo in his best voice.

Sarah just sat back and smiled as if she'd already talked with Lauren before we'd met. I didn't care. I was an activist, a shit stirrer, someone needed to do the organising.

Lauren picked up her pencil and twirled it between her fingers as a way to organise her thoughts.

"Sarah has got some good ideas about gathering community support and you two look like you're doing well on the activist side of things, so I guess my job is to get you as much exposure as possible. If I can keep up media pressure that will buy us time to make something stick" said Lauren.

"Did you see the last report on the royal commission?" I asked.

"Yep it went national in the states but it burnt out quickly as there was no more fuel for the fire. You guys are the fuel.

Keep up the pressure and I'll have more to report on. Sarah can then take advantage of the heightened community spirit and create new systems" she said.

Man, the bitch had brains. Really fucking smart I'm telling ya. Not to say that I wasn't of course. I was a different type of smart. At least I had balls, just not literally.

I sat back and took a deep breath. Lauren was waiting for a response. I just stared at her and kept nodding, trying to see the big picture that I had instigated with a dream. A dream to improve the standard of living for Aboriginal Australians once and for all. It seemed that others also shared this dream, so I had to share; just like a scotch finger biscuit parted in the middle, ready to break in halves to share with a sibling on a cold winter's morning.

This sounded like fucking magic. It was a plan that would work for sure. We had the foundations in place, now all that was needed was hard work. We were a team, and although I'd only just met Lauren, I could see the passion in her eyes. She wanted to be here and make a difference.

"So, what about that stat?" asked Sarah.

"Where do you start, I don't know which one to release as I've seen so much in this tiny little shit hole that is supposed to help people" I replied.

I looked at Banjo who had already written two stats down on a piece of paper after lunch. He handed them to me.

59% of the Australian youth detention population is Indigenous.

The Indigenous suicide rate is double that of the general population.

I passed this to Sarah who handed it onto Lauren. She was our media contact now, and a powerful one.

"God damn, are these figures correct?" asked Lauren. Sarah nodded her head.

"Ok I'll make a start on a story. I've already got some footage of inside the prison and talked to some boys. Sarah, you realise you'll lose your job over this?" Said Lauren.

"It will take them a while to work out it was me, so we have time. Whatever they did to me, they did it a long time ago" said Sarah.

A guard then opened the door and asked to speak to Sarah outside.

"You can speak here, what is it?" asked Sarah.

"Five-mile community are rioting. They're in lockdown with the gates barred" said the guard.

"What happened?" asked Sarah.

"They've been following the story on Kirra and want action. They have demands for the government" he said.

"Let's go team, this sounds like a story" said Lauren. Banjo and I agreed.

We all stood up and walked to the back entrance of the prison.

"I've got some organising to do" said Sarah as we reached the black door. "Take Lauren to five mile and show her the issues and I'll get some community support together"

"How?" I asked.

"Leave that to me, off you go" she said.

Lauren was waiting in a 4WD with her camera crew parked out in the street. We jumped in and headed for five-mile community.

Chapter Seven

Five-mile community was exactly five miles from the outskirts of Darwin. It resembled Kiranya in many ways except for the isolation of being away from the shops and local transport. Five miles doesn't seem a long way if you own a car, but when travelling on foot it can be a long way to the shops and back for a litre of milk.

5 mile went into lockdown quite often. When there was a riot or the safety of all was compromised, the community locked their doors and waited for help, which never came. The police relied on the Aboriginal patrols to take care of business even though serious crimes occurred including severe assaults, rape, torture, kidnappings and deprivation of liberty claims. Much like Kiranya, it was a world unto itself; another place to write off as unliveable, unsafe, violent, dirty and inhumane. It was home to approximately 300 Aboriginal people, dropping to 200 in the dry season when the community travelled in land to visit family.

Unlike Kiranya, this land was desired by the government to sell at the highest price. The title owners only had a 50-year special lease, and therefore only Aboriginal land until it became uninhabited. Lack of support for these communities is then a forgone conclusion to facilitate abandonment and an eventual takeover. Life is geared towards the rich and the smart, but the persistent man always wins. It's a battle of attrition, and 'who dares wins' is the catch cry.

We drove around the community twice until someone approached the gate.

"Hey you mob, we lock down" said a woman in her late 50s. I hopped out and explained that CNN were in Australia and wanted to do a story about five mile.

"Ok but not a good time to enter, plenty violence here now, plenty violence" she said.

"No worries Aunty, I'm Kiranya mob, plenty there too" I said. She unlocked the gate as three Aboriginal males were pounding down the door of a nearby house. They stopped to view the CNN car drive past then carried on with their handiwork. They were after a fella inside, calling payback for something God knows what. It could have been anything from taking his smokes to making fun of him, anything will do really when people are sniffing glue and drinking cheap straight scotch whiskey 24/7.

"Where can we go that's safe Aunty?" I asked as we drove inside. "I said not safe here! You deaf?" She asked.

I waved at her response and thought about leaving.

"Ok come my house then, let me in" she said.

I moved over and let her in the back door.

"I'm Roxy, who you white fella mob?" she asked.

"We're here from America love, how are you this fine afternoon?" Asked Lauren.

"What, what you say?" asked Roxy.

"How are you?" Asked Lauren.

A much better greeting. Short and to the point.

"Yeah good love. Go straight keep going, keep going" said Roxy flapping her hand.

Roxanne, Roxy for short was a full blood traditional owner of five mile. She was born there and so was her father. Her native language was Yolngu Matha which she spoke when in her community, then English when she had to. Her father was still alive but dying of kidney disease, as was Aunty Diane back home.

Lauren slowed down when five men approached the car.

"No bud, bad blood here, keep going until I say stop" said Roxy.

It was a difficult situation as they were standing in front of the car.

"Don't stop, go round, don't stop" she said.

Lauren managed to go around after waving at the men a few times. They quickly realised the CNN car was white fella property and walked to one side.

They would let them pass this time, but only this once and only because Aunty Roxy was in the car. She was the only person that was safe during a lockdown and could easily walk around at her own leisure. It was a time to console the heartbreak and mediate differences at a time where the effects of substance abuse dictated the outcome.

"Down back there, last house, yeah that one" said Roxy pointing her finger from the back seat.

Aunty Roxy's house was modest but clean and tidy. It had a 12-metre-high fence around it with a lock and chain on the gate. She had a pit bull terrier which moved on her command and ate whatever scraps were left over at night. She lived with her father who was dying from Kidney disease. He laid on the concrete for the best part of the day to cool his back. It feet better than a hospital bed, surrounded by other countrymen in similar circumstances. He was also an elder but had transferred all his responsibilities and decision-making power to

Roxy, who met with the community once a week to help resolve any outstanding issues, which were usually in abundance.

They parked the car and sat on the front veranda.

"You're that Kirra girl on TV ay?" Asked Roxy.

"Yep, that's me Aunty" I replied with a smile.

"You're the cause of all this shit today you know? Everyone want something better, they think government will come and rescue, now they all looking down here" said Roxy looking over her shoulder.

I had started something here, that's for sure.

They all wanted something better, but there was nothing wrong with that. When I looked around I could see the only way was up, but it was the same at my place, so I didn't judge too quickly.

"I just want what's best for our people, all of us" I replied.

Roxy looked at the camera crew then back at me.

"What you want then?" asked Roxy.

I gestured to Lauren. This was her cue.

"Can we do a story on you and the community" asked Lauren.

Roxy paused and looked at the ground.

"The last one didn't tell truth, they lie. I didn't understand all on TV but my niece told me they lie" said Roxy looking straight at Lauren.

It was true, the media had their own agenda. It was about ratings and causing alarm, not necessarily the truth.

Lauren didn't say anything.

"Ok Aunty, you have my word, no lies; just an honest report on five mile and an issue you're facing" I said.

"Look around you, what do you see?" asked Roxy.

We all scanned the environment and saw the usual community sights; camp dogs with ribs sticking out, rundown dwellings, rubbish, kids not at preschool, angry people, drunk people, hungry people and more.

"I can see Roxy, which issue can we report on first?" asked Lauren.

"What's most important one?" asked Roxy with a sly look. Lauren was sharp as a tack, so she realised it was a trick question.

"It's not what you see, that's for sure! These problems round all places. Try fix one and one more steps to take place, useless" said Aunty.

We all sat there and tried to guess what she was talking about.

"Go out there with camera and film. Everything settled now cause Kirra here. Don't talk to people, just film what you see" said Roxy.

Lauren and her crew grabbed a few cameras and split up. One went next door and filmed the grotty floor where mould had grown to look like a swamp dwelling. The kitchen was old with no hot water. There was no air conditioning and the fans were substandard. Lauren took her camera and filmed the entire community from a corner position, scanning everything in slow motion. This would be the opening shot for the story. They filmed the camp dogs, the rubbish, the empty glue containers and aerosol cans, the scotch bottles and the solemn mood that overshadowed the community. But these were only the visible images which the media craved. After all, TV is all about visibility as the volume just may be turned down at the time. If it is, one can still see the images and understand the story.

After an hour of filming we came back to her house and sat in the same position.

"What did you see?" asked Roxy.

It was a rhetorical question.

"The glue I reckon. Can't think straight with that shit in your brain" I said.

Aunty nodded

"I agree totally, absolutely yes. I think the living conditions are a close second, but that's only my humble opinion of course" said Lauren, saying much more than she had to.

We looked at Aunty as she smiled and began to giggle.

"You see anyone talking to each other?" She asked.

"We did see people fighting" Lauren replied.

"Fighting with your mouth not talking, just scream back to each other, no one listen. I've been busy with my Dad, he's sick inside. Been no one to bring community together and talk when things settle down. That's when trouble start, when no communication" said Roxy.

Aunty was highlighting the power of leadership. The one individual or group of people that can unite a land. Every community had these people but some were more effective than others.

"Come inside Kirra, give me hand" said Roxy.

I went inside with Roxy and helped her father onto the bed. He'd been lying on the concrete for too long and had become stiff as a board. This was his choice of course, but the floor was hard, really fucking hard and wasn't good for him in my opinion.

"Trying to keep him feeling good for as long as I can. He need dialysis today so I need a lift to the renal unit" said Roxy.

"You got it Aunty" I replied.

We went back outside and waited for Aunty to finish the point she was trying to make before we went inside.

She got up and walked to the front fence and began to talk.

"All this you see, all this stuff on ground, dirty places and glue everywhere is cause no talking, no leader with time to talk. I'm goanna call a community meeting in one hour. You can come with camera" said Aunty.

She reminded me of Aunty Diane back home in Kiranya, as all the male elders had passed on and left her responsible. She was sick, with no one to take her place, so there was no peacemaker or someone who could sit down and talk issues through when everything was calm. Communities need a mediator, a person who can bring people together. A person that people respect, an elder of the community....... a leader.

I made sandwiches for everyone on the front Veranda and we sat looking out onto the community. People from the next house were looking on to see what I would do next, thinking I had some kind of magic wand. What I'd learnt about change in my brief experience was that bravery was the vital ingredient. There was no magic cure, just the willingness to act in spite of being afraid.

The CNN crew were already putting their story together; clipping video footage, writing dialogue and thinking of how to capture the hearts and minds of the American public. The objective was to shock, and inform. Roxy just sat there with the world on her shoulders; worrying about the future perhaps and what lay in store for her beloved community. She looked at me as the wind blew through my hair. She had sensed something about me, something I didn't understand as well as she did. Something that could not be put into words.

Her eyes began to protrude past my outer world and into my consciousness, a deep piercing stare that somehow bestowed some kind of responsibility on me. I felt worthy of the challenge and breathed in deeply to let it into my soul, now engrained within my very disposition. She gave me something.

I didn't know what, but I felt obligated to accept it from her. The wind blew through Roxy's hair as it did mine and the moment ended. She looked away then stood up.

There was a bell under the veranda of the common room, just next to the campfire to signal when the community is required to convene. Aunty asked me to go over and give the rope a tug. It wasn't a loud bell by any means, as it seemed to clunk more than ding. We had to gather everyone house my house anyway so I think it was more symbolic than effective.

We all sat around the fire place and waited for calm, as some were still agro from the violence that caused a lock down. Everyone attended as they knew it would ease the pain. Everyone respected Aunty Roxy as the only elder of the community, and when things had settled it was time for her to talk.

"Danny boy, what was all the agro today?" Asked Roxy. Danny was a middle-aged man with drug problems and a long history of violence. He'd been in and out of prison since he was a boy.

"Dunno Aunty, that stuff just makes me crazy. Can't help it" replied Danny.

"Silvia, take the glue and grog and bring it to me later. No more pension money for him until next pay. He need to sober up" said Roxy.

Silvia was his mother who had little influence over him unless Roxy backed her up. If Danny didn't do what the elder said, then he'd be banished for a week and forced to live in a long grass community, and no one liked that. At least they had food, shelter and access to clean water in the community. Others around had it much worse, a lot fucking worse.

Danny nodded at his Mother who was standing across from him with her arms folded. She was now empowered to act with the assistance of an elder.

"Ginger, what's going on with all that yelling and screaming?

I hear you walking round for ages doing that, makes everyone sad" asked Roxy.

Ginger didn't respond. She had passed out on the ground with grief.

"Her Mum died in hospital yesterday. She in mourning period" replied Silvia.

"Why don't no one tell me? I got a right to know" Said Roxy. Roxy went on querying each person who was involved in the lock down. There was no blame, no raised voice and no anger. It was just a platform to talk with and elder present. This is what Kiranya needs, I thought. Who would take over when Aunty passes away?

I witnessed a highly effective process that made all that were present feel at ease. It was a leadership process from an Aboriginal perspective. Black fellas talking out their differences without getting locked up. Of course, there were some things out of their control, especially when an individual had committed a series crime and the police needed to get involved. The objective of this round table meeting was to intervene before those things happened. Each moment builds onto the next in a positive or negative way. The elders were the nucleus of the community and facilitated the processes that kept them all safe. Without the elders, there was no leadership, without leadership there was chaos, and with chaos brings suffering. I had learnt my lesson.

Meanwhile, Lauren was filming all of this from every possible angle. She asked Roxy whether this could be part of the story.

"It is the story love. Can't you see what I'm trying to say here?" She replied.

Lauren got it.

Instead of the whole camp dog busted house angle, there would be a new focus for the story. Roxy could've just explained what she wanted at the beginning, but we needed to find out for ourselves.

Lauren's camera crew started to pack up ready to head back into the city. They had all the footage they needed for a great story, but wanted to pay their respects to Roxy before they left.

"Thank you dear, you're a keen spirit indeed. I hope your Dad improves" said Lauren to Roxy.

"Thank you love, I like the way you talk" replied Roxy.

We all laughed and headed for the car.

I had promised Roxy a taxi ride to the hospital for her father, so I rang using Lauren's mobile phone then let her know. Just before we all left, Roxy approached me at the passenger side window to say her goodbyes.

"Kirra, go to the elders for strength, go to the Larrakia mob in town. They powerful mob. Talk to them" said Roxy.

The Larrakia Nation are the traditional owners of all land and waters of the greater Darwin area. They could help me connect to my ancestry and draw strength for the journey ahead.

"I'll get word to them that you're coming" said Roxy.

I nodded and gave her a smile.

"Christ, that was intense" said Banjo who'd been very quiet for the last two hours.

"Where've you been man?" I asked.

"Mixing with the locals. I went to school with Danny so we caught up. I stopped him from punching those fellas and brought him to the camp fire" said Banjo.

"Lauren, we're going to see the Larrakia mob in the city. I reckon me and Banjo alone this time. Personal stuff" I said.

"Look I totally understand. Sacred business is personal business. Totally cool, ok" said Lauren.

On our way to the city, we passed the long grass community just down from the cop station. We stopped to inform our CNN fiends of the situation and tried to catch a glimpse of their camp. Lauren had binoculars so she could see bodies moving and hazy like structures that resembled houses of some kind.

"Can you come back and take some footage of that?" I asked.

"Sure thing. I'll tell Sarah about this as well. Jesus Christ someone needs to do something" said Lauren.

And of course, she was right. These people were knocking on heaven's door with a sledge hammer, perhaps a wrecking ball even. They had lost all reason to live, begging God to end it all, then being promptly denied, having to persevere through the countless days and everlasting pain.

Chapter Eight

After waiting almost 30 minutes in the Burger King drive through, we arrived at Darwin city close to nightfall. It was later than expected so we had little chance of meeting the Larrakia elders who were long gone from the office. Lauren dropped us off on Cavanagh Street then retired for the night. We were on our own back near Woolworths where it all began. I remember Banjo mucking around in that alley like the Oklahoma Kiddy on horseback, and the cop cars racing towards us with sirens ablaze. Little did we know what it all meant at the time or where it would lead us? Now we were back in the thick of things and needed to wait until dawn to meet the elders. It mattered not really, as our interests lay elsewhere for the time being.

There was still one facet of Aboriginal existence that was unexplored; another world unto itself that was just as real, but not as brightly lit. A world of darkness that hid within the bright lights of Darwin city. A population of night dwellers that fed from the scraps of civilisation right under our noses. They were the city long grasses who mixed with the white homeless population, scavenging the back streets of Darwin for anything they could find, seeking refuge in the dark streets that intertwined like a rabbit warren. They were no better off than the cop station long grasses except for the convenience of inner city living where one could easily find shelter from the rain. In some ways there were more vulnerable than other fringe dwellers as they befriended the local homeless population at night. This cohort of city slicker usually carried a weapon of some sort and would not hesitate to intimidate anyone present to reach an outcome. Due to the rabbit warren nature of the city streets and the lack of police on the beat, countless unreported crimes took place each and every night. It was our intention to investigate for ourselves and report anything we saw for Lauren's story. We hoped that nothing would happen, but in the dark drug fuelled world of the long grasser, we were sure to see something.

"Hey Kirra, let's stay away from Woolworths, that Port Keats mob is still there" said Banjo.

And indeed, they were with their 4WDs still in the same position. They were sleeping the streets of Darwin as night dwellers, taking a risk to avoid accommodation fees.

"Yeah right, let's go down near Government House on the water" I replied.

This is where it all happened, night and day. This place was notorious for violent crimes, as it was poorly lit and no cops ever went there. With this combination in mind, the long grass community flocked in droves and drank until they dropped, taking the law into their own hands when a disagreement presented itself.

We had to see it for ourselves.

"Watch it Babe, keep all your weight on your back foot, that's it" said Banjo as we climbed down a sand bank to the water edge.

We reached the plateau quickly then walked around for a look. It was a fucking wasteland with long grasses pissed out of their minds. Most of them walked in a zig zag fashion, and others were passed out on the lawn. There was no lighting and no law and order to be seen. From our position, sitting on a sand stone rock, we saw multiple assaults and mixed substance abuse causing near death. One lady was sniffing glue and petrol, then drinking straight vodka to wash it all down. She walked in a snake like fashion for one minute then collapsed for about five. This went on until three men approached her who weren't much better.

"Hey Banjo, they took that girl into the bushes" I said.

"I'll go and see if she needs a hand" said Banjo.

"No fucking way I'm coming" I said.

I ran to the bushes with Banjo and saw her being pack raped. She was just lying there helpless, unable to fight back, being outmatched in every way.

"Get off her you fucking pricks!" I screamed.

Banjo ran over and jobbed one of the guys in the mouth. The others flew the coup and left their victim in the bushes to live another day. But would she? The lady had passed out and had multiple wounds to the body. They not only raped her but punched and kicked her body. She was in a real state and needed help.

Banjo pulled a mobile phone from his shorts and rang 000.

"Where did you get that?" I asked.

"This is Danny's from five mile" he said.

"You stole it? You stole Danny's phone?" I asked.

"No I borrowed it. He's cut off for the next week remember?

No money and resources by order of Aunty Roxy. I'll return it" he said.

"You'd better" I demanded.

Banjo was on the line for five minutes telling the cops what happened. He remained anonymous for obvious reasons but they didn't like that one bit. They accused him of acting suspicious and were hesitant to send a car. There were many prank callers in the area at the time. I knelt down to the victim's eye level and whispered softly.

"It's ok honey, things will get better soon" I said.

I referred to her going to hospital and receiving the treatment she deserved.

I could see her injuries close up and the pain she endured. She had experienced multiple injuries to her face, including a small slash under her eye. The guy who fled had a knife and was now at large, perhaps willing to repeat his handiwork.

"This happen every night, all night" said a short lady that approached us.

"We here not safe. Hate this place. My home I hate now. No place to live" she said.

She walked around in circles for about three minutes holding her hands in the air, wailing to the Gods for some kind of intervention that never came. She cried for herself and for her country, she shed a tear for the injured girl now laying in my arms, and wailed for peace that perhaps only death could bring. Her cries went unanswered that night, and the many nights beforehand.

It wasn't long before she tired and crawled up into a ball on the water's edge, happy to dream of the night sky and a perfect world, only to wake the next morning to find it was vanity.

I held the young girl in my arms while Banjo talked to the cops. "I fucking told you already. Were on the beach next to the Darwin chair cinema. She's been pack raped and slashed with a knife. Get down here" said Banjo.

The girl began to convulse in my arms. I felt her whole body stiffen then shake like an earthquake. This lasted for a couple of minutes before she let out a horrendous moan and went into cardiac arrest.

"Fuck she's having a heart attack, do something" I said.

"Do fucking what. I'm not a doctor" replied Banjo.

I ripped open her shirt in dramatic fashion, propelling her buttons into the night sky. I took a deep breath and positioned myself in the CPR position.

"I think I've got this right, I reckon. Oh, I don't fucking know. Banjo?" I asked.

"Yeah just do it man, start pounding" said Banjo.

I took one last look for an ambulance. I wanted to hear that sweet sound, that high pitched siren that would make everything better. The only noise I heard was my heart pounding through my chest, and quickly realised this was all on me.

"Fuck, I can do this. If I can start a movement then I can save this girls life" I said to myself.

I put my hands together, stood up on my knees and looked down at her chest. Banjo was standing behind me, breathing onto the back of my neck. I started pushing down, grunting on each thrust, not really knowing if I was helping or contributing to her death. I checked for a pulse every so often but I couldn't feel anything.

"Put your fingers together babe, right side not left" said Banjo as I felt for a pulse.

"They are and it is the left. I think I can feel something" I replied.

I continued to push hoping to get a genuine pulse.

I stopped and felt again.

"Nothing, it's gone" I said.

"Here, out the way. I'll have a go" said Banjo.

He pounded away for about three minutes before we heard the sound of an ambulance coming. Banjo picked her up in his arms and we walked down the road to meet it half way. We saw the Ambulance stop around 100 metres before us then turn around.

We yelled to the heavens.

"Hoy! Back here, back here man!!" said Banjo.

I waved my hands in the air and screamed, but it was no use. It was pitch black with screaming long grasses all around us.

I had to think if a way to flag them down.

I looked at Banjo and saw the phone sticking out of his back pocket, then grabbed it and started the flashlight function. It was the only light source around and stood out for miles.

They turned back within a couple of minutes.

We stood on the side of the road while the medics worked on her in the ambulance. They pounded her chest and used those electric shock things, whatever they're called.

"C'mon man" said Banjo unable to think of anything else to say.

What can you say? The only thing we could do was stand there and trust the system.

We waited for good news kicking small rocks onto the road to pass the time. There were mixed reactions from excitement to panic as they did everything they could to save her life. Then, silence; a deathly silence that filled our hearts with grief.

She was dead.

There was nothing more they could do to treat a massive heart attack brought on by trauma and excessive drug use. She'd been murdered and the culprits were still at large.

We both walked away from the scene crying. Banjo hid his tears by shaking his head profusely and cursing the Gods.

I just wept freely, holding my head high so the night breeze could dry the tears before they ran down my face.

We stopped in the middle of the road and held each other tight.

"Fucking hell" was all that I could say.

"We need to talk to the elders. We need to draw strength from them, just as Aunty Roxy said" said Banjo.

I nodded with my head on his chest, feeling his heart pounding, lunging at me with intent.

We walked back up the steep bank until we reached higher ground where the lights of Darwin illuminated the city streets. We walked by Government house and into the centre of Darwin to catch a bite to eat for dinner. We didn't talk much as we were still stricken from grief, wondering how many other long grasses had died that year, as that kind of news never reached the papers.

Two cop cars passed us on Mitchell Street and took a second look. They didn't stop as their sirens were flashing. We needed a place to hide out, and fast.

"Do you know anyone in the city?" I asked.

"Only Jimmy in Larrakeyah, but we've probably worn out our welcome" said Banjo.

"I heard he got charged for helping us" I said.

"They all did" replied Banjo.

We walked into the city centre where billboards lined the walls. There was paper everywhere glued on with a roller. It looked like some kind of montage with advertising from debut rock bands to breakthrough skin creams that made you look younger in two weeks. Above all of this was an electronic screen that broadcasted the news on the hour. It was around 8pm and we needed a pickup so we hung around to see the news coverage.

"Fuck" said Banjo as he looked at the screen. "It's us down on the beach"

"How the fuck did that happen?" I asked.

I looked up and saw me and Banjo trying to save the girls life in infer red. It must have been filmed by satellite. But how?

I took out Banjo's phone and gave it a once over.

"Shit, this phone has a tracer app on it" I said.

"No shit" replied Banjo.

It was Danny's phone who was sentenced to home detention. It must have activated when we left five mile, then registered at the cop station. This was a deviant back up plan when the home detention wrist bands malfunctioned. Most people take their phones everywhere with them, so when the cops apprehend someone of interest, they put a tracer app on the phone and lock it. This is common practice around these traps but extremely deceptive.

"Look, it only shows us trying to help, then waiting at the ambulance" I said looking back up at the screen.

"That's our take on it, but what about the cops?" asked Banjo.

"Do you think the police have had a change of heart? Looks like they're promoting our cause" I said.

"No fucking way, I'm wanted for kidnapping. They're trying to ruin our reputation somehow" replied Banjo.

And sure enough out came the headline for the story:

'Banjo Marlngurra is still at large in Darwin city. Here he can be seen assaulting an innocent homeless girl before fleeing the scene by foot with his girlfriend, now hostage, Kirra Yunipingu.

By this time people had gathered around the screen staring at us. Some came up and offered their support, both white and black. Some offered us money, others wanted to help any way they could. Support came from all directions except from the law enforcement agency who swore to defend and uphold the truth.

"Banjo, did you turn that phone off" I asked.

"Shit…. yes, there we go, all good" replied Banjo.

It was too late. The cops had pin pointed our exact position and sent out the dogs. Cop cars came racing down Darwin Street Mall in sets of three at a time from both directions, hoping to sandwich us in the middle. A helicopter then flew over and shone a spotlight on us.

"Lay down with your hands up" said the cop from high above.

I put up my middle finger and so did Banjo. We must've looked beautiful from up there, standing tall with a look of self-determination in our eyes and a middle finger made of steel. I felt like Napoleon ready for battle with only a 'fuck you' as ammunition. These pigs didn't stand a chance.

"Kirra, this way man, to the alley that leads to Cavanagh Street. Let's go Babe" said Banjo.

I followed his lead. As long as he didn't pull me through another iron fence I'd be happy.

We ran like fugitives up the middle of the road, parting the cars that travelled to and from the city. The bitumen seemed to get harder with every ten metres as our ankles succumbed to the pressure. We rested and looked to the left and right. St. Paul's church was just ahead so we ran a bit further and entered the front doors. Inside was a Catholic Priest lighting candles around the alter. He turned around looking puzzled as the cop cars approached from both directions outside.

"Sanctuary! We need sanctuary" I cried.

"My dear girl, Sanctuary was abolished many years ago. We have no foundation to protect you" said the Priest.

I was careful not to swear.

"Stiff, lock the doors and call sanctuary. Do you know who we are?" I asked.

"It matters not, all are equal in Gods eyes" said the Priest. Shit, I thought I heard that in a movie somewhere. I didn't care about what God thought, I just wanted his help then I'd be on my way. I locked the doors myself as the priest and Banjo looked on.

"What the flopping heck are you doing?" Asked Banjo.

"Saving our buts. We'll call sanctuary and fool the cops. Father...sorry what's your name?" I asked.

"Father Clementine my child" he said.

"I assume you are familiar with the Catholic involvement in the stolen generation?" I asked.

"Excuse me?" He said.

"The removal of Aboriginal children and placed in Catholic missions?" I asked.

He paused and thought long and hard before responding.

"I am" he replied.

"Then you need to help. This is pay back, now help lock all the doors and windows" I demanded.

He moved towards the far end windows and bolted each one, then helped Banjo bolt the front doors.

The cops banged on the main doors and demanded entry.

"Open up in the name of the law" said a familiar voice. It was senior sergeant detective Edwards. He was loud and straight to the point.

"Open up Banjo, this is where it ends. Give up and we'll go easy on you" he said from behind the door.

"Sanctuary! We have asylum in here" I said.

Of course, we didn't but it sounded good, and it was the only playing card I had.

We didn't hear anything for about ten minutes. They must have been checking if our clam was valid. Edwards was a smart cop, but he needed to check every detail before making a move. He was thorough but a little blind to reality when it counted.

Sgt Edwards spoke on the loud speaker from outside.

"Banjo and Kirra, I'd like to speak with you alone" he said.

I wasn't going to let him in. As soon as he had access he'd call in the foot soldiers. There's no way I was falling for that one.

"Babe, let's take a stand. Right here right now" said Banjo.

"I don't wanna get caught in here forever" I replied.

"That's not what I mean. Make some demands babe. Get some people together who can take over what you've begun" said Banjo.

"I think what your friend is trying to say is that you should call in a team of some sort" said Father Clementine.

"Yes that's it Minister. A team" said Banjo.

I thought for a minute before speaking.

An A-Team (Aboriginal Team) perhaps to carve a new future. It had to be made up of key players or it would be a waste of time.

"Who then?" I asked.

"May I suggest representation from all the nooks, corners and crannies of society young lady" Said Father.

"What?" I replied.

"Perhaps the Chief Minister, A Larrakia elder, the Darwin Lord Mayor and someone from the clergy" said Father.

"Meaning you?" I asked.

"Happy to oblige miss" he replied.

"And what powers would the A-Team have?" I asked Father.

"It matters not at this stage. Just to form a task force powerful enough to make major decisions is progress enough" he said. It was all starting to make sense. I was but a spark in this whole fireplace of issues. I was the seed of change, not the change itself. Banjo looked and me and nodded. He understood more than he let on.

It was all just too surreal. How could a 17-year-old skinny Aboriginal girl get into this mess and be asked to clean it up herself? It just didn't seem fair. I felt obligated to help but I was out of my depth, although I'd only just learnt to swim a few days ago.

Father was onto something. Otherwise what was all this commotion for? Did I want to end up in the clink and forgotten about in a month? I didn't want to become just another statistic. It was all or nothing, it was time to take a stand.

I yelled my demands out the front door for all to hear. The local media were there by that stage as well as Lauren and her CNN camera crew. They were set to get some major international coverage, which now included the Catholic Church. I hoped that Father wouldn't get into trouble.

Chapter Nine

No one in Darwin was quite prepared for what would happen in the coming days. I had demanded that certain people, very influential people, attend the church at 9am the next morning to discuss the formation of a new body; an A-Team specifically designed to come up with solutions to the most difficult problems, with measurable outcomes independently assessed by the United Nations. This meant that one government or any one body couldn't just talk up their performance to get re-elected or receive their grant money. This would be an A-Team of accountability and above all, action. It would be a team with strong legislative powers, bound by a strict code of ethics and stringent guidelines outlining its powers. Some would say it's just one more group that talks, one more hoop to jump through before going nowhere, but I say different. I see my people killing themselves every day, some slow, others quick, like the long grasses at the cop station, or Banjo's father. It happens every day and we need someone who can make good decisions without being hindered. My people deserved change, and I intended to see that they had it.

The media were the only ones who stayed after the entourage of cops left for the night. The front door was guarded by one uniformed police officer who stood out on the pavement smoking a cigarette. CNN coverage across America had been immense. The average American sympathised with our cause and voiced their concerns on air. From Los Angeles to New York and across Canada, they wanted to know who I was and what I intended to do. This is why I now had Lauren outside beating down the church door wanting yet another interview. I let them in and saw the cop outside drinking coffee on a small park bench; he'd settled in for the night.

Lauren brought hamburgers and coffee in for me and Banjo. I shared mine with Father who ate slowly, looking slightly confused after each mouthful. I think he was a vegetarian, but he didn't want to dampen the atmosphere. He was a kind man that had dedicated his life to the church. I had dedicated mine to my people. We had a lot in common.

Lauren suggested the interview be called 'sanctuary for human rights' and held near the alter to give it a religious feel. This story would be beamed across 200 countries, detailing the plight of Aboriginal people and what lay in store as a result of our little adventure. I was hoping for change, real long-lasting change. I had faith in the power of one, but confidence in the power of the collective that seemed to dwarf whatever best intentions I had. I knew that I would need to walk away from all this at some stage and let others take over, and I knew that I wouldn't agree with some of the decisions they made. But I had faith in the here and now and the difference I could make.

Lauren and her crew were busy setting up near the alter under the guidance of Father Clementine, while I put on my make up for the interview. The only time I'd worn pancake and eye shadow was at school in 'girls business' where we all got together and talked about the issues of womanhood. Most of us knew about sex, puberty and everything else through life experience, so the counsellor just brought in makeup and gave us a demo. We couldn't learn this from life experience as the shop keepers at Casuarina Square wouldn't let us into their businesses, as they knew we didn't have any money. I remember walking by the most popular boutiques and seeing the white girls sampling the many shades of mascara and eye shadow, whilst the poor black girls were given the devils eye for even walking past. I didn't actually give a fuck as my black skin glistened in the sun after washing my face with plain water. That's all I needed to look like a genuine person. At least I thought so. But this was television and I was told that a little makeup would be needed.

Banjo looked upon proceedings with a dubious look in his eye. I could tell what he was thinking even when I wasn't looking at him. This is the trade mark of a soul mate I guess or as I say 'my fella' in plain English.

"You look different" said Banjo as I turned and looked at him with a touch of foundation on my cheeks.

I think it actually enhanced my facial features, which is what Banjo was trying to say.

"I mean, you look…different" he said again.

"Don't get fucking mushy bro" I said with a chuckle to disguise my embarrassment.

We both laughed at each other as the makeup artist tried to finish her handiwork ready for the interview.

The makeup artist gave me a once over, then told me to keep my head still and look straight ahead. After a few last 'dabs' of her sponge and a look in the mirror, we were done. All that was needed now was a scene of pure serenity.

"My child, look at my Church. It's now a mockery. Please tell me that you have something worthwhile to say?" Said Father Clementine.

"I'm sorry, but this is important. I'll ask for the lights to be dimmed around the alter" I replied.

"No that's fine. I guess I'm just feeling a little nervous about all this and perhaps how the Pope will react seeing live coverage in Rome" he said.

"I'm sure he'll take it well" I replied, knowing nothing about the clergy and the politics involved.

He nodded and began to pace up and down the aisle whispering "give me strength lord, give me strength"

"Kirra, it's time" said Lauren.

I stood up and looked at Banjo. He hadn't taken his eyes off me for thirty minutes so he didn't need say anything in support. Just a nod to set me on my way to change the world.

I sat with my legs crossed opposite Lauren. She wore an elegant navy-blue business suit that put my tourist outfit to shame. It was ok though as I was me, just myself discussing real issues that affected my people. I guess the somewhat ragged look added to the appeal of a desperate race that needed real solutions.

The lights were the most daunting part of the scenery as they shone almost directly in my eyes. It's hard to tell from the camera, but it was blinding. I was told not to look at the lights and keep my attention on Lauren. The interview started formally which made me pep up and speak the best I could. It meant the Queen's English, if that was possible.

"Kirra, the world is watching you tonight. The viewers have undoubtedly heard of your plight. In your own words, what would you like to see change in Australia?" asked Lauren.

"I just want a fair go for my people. Australian Aboriginals deserve access to basic living standards just like everyone else" I replied.

"So what can the average Australian do to help you?" she asked.

"These issues are so big that no one government or body is capable of fixing them alone. We need the whole Australian community behind us to play their part" I said.

"And what could that look like, give us an example" she said. I was put on the spot, but it was ok. I'd started this, so I needed to explain further.

"If someone sees and injustice they usually think that someone else is doing something about it. Take it on yourself to act. This could mean to donate some of your time, buy someone a bite to eat, anything really. These issues belong to all Australians and only a whole community approach will fix them" I said.

Lauren brewed over her notebook.

"But Kirra, can you see that most Australians would feel shame over this and avoid the issues at all cost. After all, the natural reaction is to avoid in these circumstances" she asked.

"Yeah I get that" I replied.

Shit I said yeah.

"But when the first few act then others will see what's possible. Because others have made a difference they will see the results and act as well. It's a domino effect, but the first few dominos are the most important because they will determine what's possible" I said.

"Kirra, I believe that's already happened. We've got some footage of something you'll be interested in" said Lauren.

I looked at the plasma TV that was set up on the alter before a row of lit candles. Kiranya then emerged onto the screen showing the wider community cleaning up rubbish, sweeping verandas, painting walls and constructing a fence around the perimeter. I saw senior sergeant Edwards training Aboriginal security guards at the front entrance and shaking their hands. I saw unlawful people being sent away when their behaviour reached an unacceptable level. I saw a community at peace, but above all, I saw the community collaborate with black and white working together to change the world. I began to cry. The tears swelled in my eyes as the camera took a close up. I could feel a million hearts bleed through the camera as I turned my gaze from the screen to Lauren. I could tell that Sarah was the main driver behind this movement but was surprised that Sgt Edwards had also played a part. Perhaps that's what he wanted to discuss with me at the cop shop? Perhaps that's who opened the gate and let us out? He was playing the good cop bad cop routine to our advantage.

The interview ended with smiles all round. The right questions bad been asked and the rating numbers were through the roof.

"Five million CNN viewers Kirra. This will also be beamed across all major Australian TV channels as well as the BBC. By this time tomorrow over 20 million People will know what's happened here" said Lauren.

I couldn't believe it. Was this a dream come true or just one in the making? I was pretty sure it was the latter and quickly realised that I still had unfinished business before I retired at the ripe old age of 17. I just wanted to get back to my community to see the difference I'd made, but how long would this last? I had to get the A-Team together and leave a legacy, but now it was time to rest.

"Thank you, Kirra," said Lauren as she walked outside with her camera crew.

The cop was still there on the bench. He'd watched the live coverage on his phone and I could tell he was moved. He caught my attention and walked across the road towards a long grass countryman who was passed out on the footpath. He didn't perform a miracle or give him $100 or anything. He simply helped him up and called the homeless shelter to come and pick him up. There he would have a bed for the night and get something to eat. It was all he could do but it was enough.

It was one kind act from a community member that could encourage others to do the same.

"Got that" said Lauren from behind me holding a camera. "Great footage. I'll use it for another story early next week. Stay here until the A-team arrive then get their support. They will then have influence over the police commissioner who has the power to drop the charges" said Lauren.

I leant over and gave her a hug as she patted me on the back. I wanted to hug Sarah as well. I turned around and locked the door as Father and Banjo blew out half the candles.

"Good night my children. There are two beds in the upper hall where you can retire. I will see you at 8am tomorrow morning" Said Father.

We thanked him for everything and waved goodnight. It was just me and Banjo left, standing before the alter with the candles flickering our shadows onto the wall. We held each other and took sanctuary in one another's arms. We were careful not to sin in God's presence although we did have a lot to celebrate, but this was no place to show disrespect.

We walked outside and sat on the courtyard lawn. It was well protected from the public with only a small gate in which to enter from the outside. It was open, just like the gate at the lock up that night. We looked around and saw two men sitting cross legged in the corner. One lit a cigarette lighter.

"Sit down Kirra" said a man sitting cross legged. We moved closer and saw two Aboriginal men with white sandstone paint spread over their chests and arms. They were elders from the Larrakia Nation and it was time to pay our respects and draw strength for the day ahead.

We sat down cross legged before the elders.

"My name is Galarrwuy, he is Jagera. We are leaders from the Larrakia Nation. You must be proud?" said Galarrwuy.

"We are, but there is more to do" I said.

"There always is. I saw the local news footage and the answer is yes", he said.

"Yes to what?" I asked.

"I will be a part of the A-Team as you call it. But first you need to draw strength from your ancestors and the spirits who inhabit this land" said Galarrwuy.

He stood up and made a fire in the middle of the lawn. He used a flint and splinters of fine bark wood, then added kindling to create a temporary fire to suit his purpose.

We crossed our legs around the fire as both elders used tapping sticks to create a rhythm for their song. They sung of sea serpents riding by horseback through the escarpment landscape. They sung of war and peace, land rights and treaties, they sung of hope and wisdom. I looked into the fire and gazed at the flames that burned so brightly, and saw Mimi spirits dancing along the wood then disappearing into the flames. They were thin stick like spirits, happy to be summoned into the world of the living and share the joy. They danced for me and Banjo, they danced for the future and for the sheer enjoyment of dancing itself. I gazed into the fire and began to feel a deep sleep overwhelm me. I saw brotherhood, unity and love. I saw happy communities thriving under strong Aboriginal leadership. I saw understanding. I saw me. It was a vision of how things could be, not necessarily the future. The spirits had shown me what was possible, not what would occur. They had simply shown the way and inspired me to keep going.

"What you saw is for you alone Kirra. Take it and do what's right" said Galarrwuy.

I looked at Banjo and we embraced. I needed his strength as I couldn't do it alone. With the help of my man, the community and the spirits, I would ensure lasting change.

We turned back around to find the elders gone and the fire extinguished. They had given us hope and strength for the coming day. We had also paid our respects to the traditional owners of the Darwin area.

We ventured back inside and retired to our room. It was a simple bedroom with a crucifix on the wall and a small pitcher of water in the corner. Simplicity was the theme of the room and indeed the church as a whole. I took this on board as the theme of tomorrow's meeting. To keep it simple would be the best way forward, and Banjo agreed.

Chapter Ten

Father Clementine opened our door at 8am with coffee and toast on a tray. We sat up in bed and ate hearty ready for the day ahead.

"Thanks Father, you're a saint" I said, trying not to be sarcastic.

He smiled and returned after we'd finished and collected the trays. We found our tourist clothes freshly washed and ironed at the base of our beds; Father had risen early to do whatever he could to help. We wondered what we could do to repay his generosity. We had nothing to give but kindness and a thankful nature.

"We can pray with him, he'd like that" said Banjo.

"But we're not Christians" I answered.

"I guess, but look at all the people who've changed their views to our benefit. You saw the news footage last night. People who had never even come to Kiranya before are now helping to turn it around. It's the least we can do for him I reckon" said Banjo.

I nodded and got dressed. We met Father downstairs, took his hand and led him to the alter. He stood between us and wondered what we were doing, looking left then right with an inquisitive smile. I took the lead and knelt before God and put my hands together, as they did soon afterwards. It was a serene experience, like connecting with the Mimi spirits and receiving guidance for the day ahead. Anyway, Father was happy as we had repaid his kindness.

"Thank you, my children. God bless you" he said to us.

It was nearing 9am and we were getting nervous, especially Father who continually rubbed his crucifix neck chain every chance he could. I was looking out the stain glass windows every few minutes or so, somewhat expecting Sgt Edwards to come back with his pack of wild dogs and clear us out, although I assumed if this was the case, he would've made his move already. There were no guarantees in life so I just waited with a positive frame of mind.

"They will come my dear, they will come" said Father. And he was right.

At 9am precisely they drove up in a black Mercedes looking like mob guys of sort. I held my breath as the first person exited the car, then the second and so forth. My demands had been met and I was a happy girl.

The first person to walk up the steps was the Lord Mayor of Darwin Sally Nguyen then the Chief Minister of the Northern Territory David Marshall, Galarrwuy Namatjira elder of the Larrakia Nation and Father Clementine who was already inside. I opened the door to greet them and was confronted by Sgt Edwards.

"Who invited you? This wasn't the deal" I said.

I tried to close the door quickly but it was too heavy. He placed his whole body between me and the door and looked me in the eye.

"If I don't enter, you and your boyfriend go to jail" said Sgt Edwards.

What could I do? He was practically inside anyway and I couldn't ask anything more of Father.

"Is it true you helped my community?" I asked.

"How do you mean? He asked.

"I saw on the news that you rallied the public and helped clean things up at Karinya" I said.

"Let's talk about it inside" he said.

I welcomed everyone in and led them to a room at the back of the church. We all sat and Father spoke.

"Thank you for meeting Kirra's request on such short notice. As this is a house of God I assume that you have no weapons at your disposal?" Looking at Sgt Edwards.

"I am unarmed" he said.

The Chief Minister was squirming in his seat, waiting to speak. "Kirra, as you are aware your boyfriend has been accused of kidnapping and assault. This is a sensitive case so I have managed to get the charges dropped as Sgt Edwards is of the opinion the allegations are false" said Chief Minister Marshall.

"That's correct Chief Minister, our investigations have concluded in that manner" said Sgt Edwards.

"Then what was that shit on the TV last night?" I asked.

"We don't have control over the media. The tracking app is a joint venture between multiple government departments. Something must have leaked" he said.

"Sounds like the government has caved in" I said. There was no response.

"So Kirra, in the matter for which we are here, in what manner are we to act? I mean, if we reside over every Indigenous issue over the land there will be hell to pay. Do you know how many departments and Aboriginal governing bodies there are in Australia?" Asked the Lord Mayor.

"The A-team would be a task force as such, not a body to tell everyone what to do. A group to make major life changing decisions, create new projects and allocate major capital. The areas would be education, health care, trauma counselling, suicide prevention, incarceration and unemployment. You would act from your own legislation with performance outcomes measured by the United Nations" I said.

"Holy shit" said the Chief Minister. "Do you know what kind of rift that would cause in the government? Another governing body to pay and separate legislation to create and enact in parliament? Kirra, be reasonable" he said.

"Chief Minister, with all the stats I've released in the media which ones are false?" I asked.

"None of them" he replied.

"And which ones have improved over the years" I asked.

"None of them" he replied.

"Exactly, none of them. If you want a different result using the same strategies then you're going about things the wrong way. We need radical ideas to create radical change. The effect of all this media coverage won't last forever, and that means the community will eventually forget we exist again. We need you lot to act and carve new ways that STICK!" I said.

"You have my full support" said Father Clementine.

"I'm in, but it won't be easy" said the Chief Minister.

Everyone else looked around the table and nodded. We had agreed on principle, but it would take time to organise.

"Father, Lauren is waiting outside to interview you all. Can you take them to the front lawn?" I asked.

"Of course," said Father.

This was necessary to document all that had been discussed and have them agree on camera. I trusted them but to have a live recorded agreement meant certain action.

As they left the church I and Banjo embraced. Never before had there been such a commitment made by so many powerful people. Never before had so many community members rallied for change. Never before had the community pitched in to help the needy. By all reports, Karinya was now unrecognisable. I couldn't wait to return and see Aunty Diane once more and embrace her on the front lawn. I was proud of the community, I was proud of my friends and family, I was proud of Banjo, and of myself.

We walked out the back door hoping to bypass the media and catch a bus home. We had done all that we could to ensure that change would flow on through the ages, which included keeping in touch with Lauren to report any attempt to renege on our agreement. It was fucking magic.

Then suddenly a cop car drove towards us at slow speed. The A-Team were still being interviewed on the front lawn of the church so the cop in the car didn't want to cause alarm.

"Hey Kirra, I need to take you to hospital" said the cop.

"Why, what's happened?" I asked.

"Your Aunty is sick" he said.

"Aunty Diane? Aunty Diane is sick?" I asked.

"That's right, jump in, I'll give you a police escort" he said.

The police car sped down Cavanagh Street then up the Stuart Highway towards the hospital. There were civilians who recognised us in the back seat and began to pursue us to offer a hand. When they caught up to us we simply waved them on.

"We're ok, no worries mate" I said to a concerned citizen.

The cop laughed.

We arrived at the Hospital at the emergency unit. I thanked the police officer and went in and asked for Aunty Diane.

"She's in intensive care" said the Doctor.

Aunty had been battling kidney disease for some time after a good twenty years of heavy drinking. This was common in my community, as it is everywhere. We went upstairs and saw her in the renal unit. It was crammed with Aboriginal people in pain. Their ankles and feet were swollen, with most unable to talk or stay off dialysis for long enough to walk around the bed. There was so much pain in the room, so much heartache and regret, so much love that would never be shared with their family. Their poison was alcohol; excessive drinking on a daily basis that included a 'drink until you drop' mentality. Their hearts were broken and the grog was their antidote; a remedy that would never reach its objective.

Aunty Diane's bed was in the east wing alongside five others with the same condition. I walked in and saw her eyes in the darkness. They looked like yellow cats' eyes peering into the night. Her jaundice had worsened and her feet were now so swollen that she couldn't wear socks.

I ran over and hugged her in bed.

"Aunty Diane, I'm sorry" I said.

"Sorry for what dear, I'm happy" she said.

"Why?" I asked.

"I'm happy for you, happy for my people. I've been watching you on TV. You famous, you too Banjo. I'm proud" she said. I looked up at the TV screen and saw the A-Team being interviewed on the lawn of St. Paul's church. Father looked nervous as did the Chief Minister, taking the credit for our 'task force' approach. I didn't care, I just wanted things to change.

"Those people gonna to do all that?" asked Aunty.

"Yep, and more. We've got the support of the community to help those who need it the most. Did you hear about Kiranya?" I asked.

"Yeah, tidy as with no humbug anymore. Well done girl, you'll sleep better at night" said Aunty.

We watched live CNN coverage and the Darwin news lying in bed together.

"Look at that young girl with makeup, who that girl?' asked Aunty giggling at the same time.

"You see how my face isn't shiny there. Much better for the camera" I replied.

I was now an expert makeup artist and planned to buy some pretty soon. After all, can't a girl look good on and off camera?

My plans for the future didn't stop there; I was so eager to get back to Kiranya and see how the community had changed for the better. I had great expectations, sincere intentions and a heart full of hope, but this moment belonged to Aunty. She was sick and needed support. All the money and intervention in the world couldn't turn back time and take away all the grog, trauma and heartbreak she'd suffered.

"Hey Aunty, where you been so long" said a familiar voice from the doorway.

It was Jimmy. He'd torn himself away from the television set to visit. He looked at me with a smile being careful not to swear in front of Aunty.

"Hey Aunty, seen better days love? How are ya?" Asked Jimmy as he gave her a kiss on the forehead.

Aunty smiled to return the gesture.

"No Seinfeld here boy, just news" I said to Jimmy.

"All good news too by the look" replied Jimmy looking up at the TV screen.

He took a seat in the corner and relaxed as I got up and drew the partition curtain for some privacy.

"Hello, Kirra are you there?" said someone from behind the curtain.

"Ahhh, Sarah!" I said as I leapt from the bed and into her arms. "You're a miracle lady, how did you work it?" I asked.

"You did it, not me" replied Sarah.

She was a modest lady who worked tirelessly behind the scenes to get results. There were a lot of people like that in the community, and she was good at finding them.

"Aunty, how are you?" Asked Sarah with an empathetic tone.

At this stage Aunty only had the strength to nod, and she didn't like to repeat herself at the best of times.

After around thirty minutes of watching CNN reruns it was time to give Aunty a rest. She was still in pain and due for another dialysis session in an hour. She was also nervous about the needles and the prospect of putting up with even more pain than she had endured. It was a difficult situation, as the pain she suffered was replaced by a different kind of pain, in which she was told would make her better. She had trouble understanding that, but then again, so did I.

"Kirra, can you stay?" asked Aunty.

"Sure" I said as the others left the room.

"You talked to the elders, the Larrakia people?" asked Aunty.

"I did. I saw the Mimi spirits Aunty. They danced for me in the fire and lifted their spears to the night sky" I replied lying next to her.

"What you think it means?" she asked.

"I'm not sure. Perhaps…to spread my wings and fly maybe? What does it mean?" I asked.

"When the Mimi spirits point their spear to the sky it means they have chosen you for something. It can be small or big, but remember important things can be small too. Did you go to sleep at the fire?" She asked.

"I did. I dreamt of the wind blowing through the Pandanas trees in Karinya. I saw the sandstone rock on the beach and the hermit crabs in the sand. They danced for me from

side to side and snapped their claws. I was dancing with them"
I replied.

"You see, environment is a good teacher. Something to do
with home then. You must return to Karinya; there you need
to be strong leader or things go back to same. Sarah and others
are not Karinya blood, that's you. You must lead" said Aunty.

"I'm only 17, I'm just a kid. You'll get better Aunty, the
doctors here are ok, they'll make you better. You'll see" I said.

Fear was getting the better of me. It would be nice to walk
away from what I had created and expect others to carry on. It
would be easier to just sit back and expect everyone to do the
work. I needed to take responsibility for what I'd created. A
bit like having children I guess, although that was on the back
burner for now.

"It's you Kirra. You must lead now. My time already gone.
It's you" said Aunty.

I swallowed a mouth full of saliva and laid back on the
pillow. I stared at the bland hospital ceiling and closed my eyes.
I could still see the Mimi spirits dancing in the fire with their
spears pointed to the stars. Perhaps I had no choice? Perhaps it
was destiny? Or perhaps it was change created out of sheer grit
and self-determination. I now understood what I was taught
at high school. Self Determination was more than just a catch
phrase to make the academics sound good and to justify their
high salaries. It was the key to creating change and improving
life for the better. But it's not something that can be just said
out loud, it needs to be proven by the amount of dirt under the
fingernails, by the tone in your voice, and the resilience in your
attitude. These are the attributes of self-determination which I
didn't hear about at school. I guess I had to learn it for myself.

"Ok then, I'll go back this afternoon. Do you need to
contact them before I get there?" I asked.

"What do you mean?" She asked.

"Well, they need to know that I'm in charge now" I said. Aunty laughed.

"If anyone need to say they're in charge then they're not in charge. That not decided by me. That decision is with the spirits. When you go back you'll understand" said Aunty.

I wanted to understand now, but I guess the most important things are not decided by us.

"Aunty Diane, time for your dialysis" said the doctor as she walked in with the machine and a packet of needles.

"You go dear, I don't want you to see me like this" she said. I knew that people can live on dialysis for years, but it was hard leaving her side. The pain she endured was also my pain. It was the emotional low when a loved one is sick and could potentially die. I wanted to stay the night and comfort her. I wanted to make the pain go away, as if she felt better, then so would I.

"Go Kirra, go to Kiranya" she said.

I left the room crying and immediately looked for Banjo. He was sitting right outside and heard everything.

"What's up babe, where are we going?" He asked.

"Home, we're going home" I replied.

We sat at the bus stop in front of the hospital and waited for around twenty minutes. All we could see were black fellas sprawled across the concrete: lying down, in wheelchairs, walking with a drip in their arm bandaged from head to toe. Their injuries were severe and vast including knife wounds, glass cuts, alcohol poisoning, broken limbs and more. It was too much for the hospital to handle at the best of times. This reduced the overall quality of service, and it also highlighted the problems I was trying to fix. It hit home. Change would come slow, and there was more work to be done. A lot more.

We got off at bus stop number 21 in front of Woolworths in Nightcliff and walked inside with our heads held high. We received numerous high fives and 'good on ya brother' compliments before we sat down at the local bakery. Banjo still hand five dollars left from the prize money that he kept in his sock, so we could buy a pie. As we ate half a pie each, Anna came over and offered her compliments.

"You fucking crazy bastards. You crack me up I'm telling ya. I guess that prize started it all eh? So I deserve part of the credit I reckon?" asked Anna.

"Too fucking right. Come here girl" said Banjo.

Anna leaned over and received her thank you kiss. It was on the cheek so I didn't mind that much. She did set the whole thing up by rigging the lottery so I guess she deserved a peck, but no fucking more. Banjo was my man and I planned to keep it that way. Don't fuck with a black fella lady in this regard I'm telling ya.

I finished my pie and laid my head on the table.

"I'm tired" I said.

"Tired? You're only metres away from a new world. Don't you want to see what's changed at Karinya?' Asked Banjo.

I did, but I guess I was just nervous. I needed to get up, but my legs wouldn't let me.

"Get up you" said Banjo as he lifted me by the arm.

This was the pickup I needed, literally.

We walked out the side door and looked for an opening in the fence.

"Where's our side escape? Who's gone and plugged it up?" Asked Banjo.

All the holes had been repaired with the whole fence extended in height to 12 metres. The only entrance was out front. We walked around and saw two security guards standing tall. It was Arnold and Johnny, two Kiranya lads who'd managed to finish high school and get an average resume together.

"Welcome home man" said Johnny.

We smiled and gave both of them a hug. They were big boys and had training from the cops, so we were confident they could handle themselves. This would work well, as if the trouble makers were denied entry, then disturbances could be kept to a minimum.

"Sgt Edwards organised all that" I said to Banjo.

Banjo nodded. He was grateful.

We walked around and saw the many changes to the environment; a 12-metre-high fence now surrounded the community with tangled barbed wire at the top. No one was getting over that in a hurry. The grass had been cut and watered, and the houses cleaned up and painted throughout. There was a fresh feel about the place that came about by two locals who took a stand. It wasn't perfect and definitely not like those million-dollar houses next to us, but it was clean and safe. I didn't have a single dollar in my pocket that day, but I felt like a millionaire.

We walked into our old house and looked around. There was some special treatment given out here I reckon, as we had a new kitchen, a flash new bed and fresh paint on the walls. My bedroom door had been fixed with putty on the back door to fill up the dents left by Banjo's baseball bat, as he fended off drunk men in the dead of the night. All these generous people who'd come to help deserved a medal. All they needed was to know the truth and see the issues drawn into the light from the darkness of the urban shadows. I went outside and sat on the front Veranda with Banjo and looked out onto the footy field. The grass was green and freshly cut with a new boundary line painted just yesterday. I looked at the Pandanus trees blowing in the wind and heard the surf break onto the sandstone rocks on the beach. I saw last night's fire out front with smouldering embers that reminded me of the Mimi spirits and how they danced that night under the starry sky. I saw five girls going to school dressed in their new uniforms bought just yesterday. They walked past and waved.

"Good morning Aunty Kirra" they said to me.

About the Author

Paul Drewitt is an Australian based writer of poetry, short stories and crime fiction novels. His work is known as being creative and forthright, always telling a worthwhile story that engages the senses and tweaks the mind. Paul does his best writing on the beach, in a library and at home in sunny Darwin, Australia.

When he isn't reading or writing, he's probably playing chess, watching Seinfeld or planning that perfect lesson to teach his high school class. He is a proud Senior Teacher who mentors others to achieve their life long goals; an occupation like no other in the world.

Paul lives in the Northern Territory of Australia with his partner and three children, a medium-sized dog and a black cat.

www.ingramcontent.com/pod-product-compliance
Lightning Source LLC
Chambersburg PA
CBHW020022030726
47499CB00007B/2223